New Hampshire
Goddess Chronicles
Volume 1

Light Your Torch!

An entertaining and informative guidebook to
beginner's feminine spirituality.

R. M. Allen

Peapod Press • Exeter, N.H.
2011

Peapod Press
An Imprint of PublishingWorks, Inc.,
151 Epping Road
Exeter, NH 03833
603-778-9883

Designed by: Melodica Design

LCCN: 2011921567
ISBN-13: 978-1-935557-64-7

New Hampshire
Goddess Chronicles

Light Your Torch!

Many thanks to the people who helped with editing: Kelley Allen, Susan Bonenfant, Beverly Caldon, Maren Tirabassi, Jeremy Townsend, and Susun Weed.

This book is dedicated to my mother,
Florence, and to the mother of us all, Mother Earth

Introduction

There comes a certain time in a woman's life when she may feel stale, outdated, and know it is time to reinvent herself. She may be at a fork in the path. She may wonder if all she has experienced so far is all there is. She may wonder the biggest question of all—what is the meaning of life? So many questions! While this book gives no concrete answers to those questions, it can be used as a beginner's guidebook to help you to find your own way. I have written with the hope that you may find your own intuitive inner goddess, or feminine power. A fun deck of Goddess Oracle Cards, by Dr. Doreen Virtue, is the vehicle for this journey. The Torch-Time exercises interspersed within introduce you to some goddesses, and are intended to help you to develop your intuition.

As the famous mythologist Joseph Campbell often said, you must "follow your bliss." "To each their own," I say. You may find your own inner goddess through the Catholic Church, a Hindu retreat, reading tea leaves, or in your own backyard herb garden. Or you may get your own deck of goddess cards and join me on the long brown path, lit by goddess torches. The point is to be receptive to new experiences, and to let those experiences open your heart, and in there, patiently waiting, you will find your own intuitive inner goddess. Wait 'til you hear what she has to say to you!

In no way does this constitute a new religion. This book will not solve all your problems. I simply hold myself up as a mirror in which you may seek your own reflection. This story is about an ordinary woman on an orgasmagical spiritual safari. It might make you laugh, it might make you cry. There are scary parts too, but you can safely follow along through the cosmos from the comfort of your couch or beach towel. Have fun, and enjoy the journey!

Part One:
Mind Games

Light Your Torch!

You are invited to follow me on a winding spiritual journey taken on the planet earth (mostly), on the North American continent, in the fine state of "Live Free or Die" New Hampshire. I invite you to join with me as I use the guidelines of Voluntary Simplicity while investigating the hidden nooks and crevices of personal spirituality. You may see flickering shadows of yourself in my tale. Or you may find yourself brightly mirrored in me or my many friends (soon to be your friends)— a group of women mischievously named The Goddesses. We are together on Walt Whitman's long brown path, (from his poem "Song of the Open Road") leading where we chose. *Allons*, grab your goddess torch and fall in line. If you are a male this will be quite voyeuristic for you, but still I invite you along. Get ready to join us on our journey in this sneaky universe that has hidden surprises all along the way. Try not to miss these synchronicities— they can be hidden quite well. When we come upon one we all say at once "what luck!" You chime in too, say it out loud, and when it gets really fun scream "Boom-shaka-Lucka!" Ok ready? Spark up your goddess torch and bring some extra matches and a plastic poncho, it might get crazy out there in the raw and untamed universe.

Church Office Interview

Did I mention that I work in a church office? I thought this very odd at first, but I think I have grown into it quite nicely. Let me tell you a little about myself. I am a typical single woman who works part-time, and has two teenage daughters. My driver's license will show you that I am Marie, a petite brunette with blue eyes, who, because of my stature, is sometimes mistaken as a child. My sun sign is Scorpio, with a Gemini moon. I am of typical hardy New England stock: French-Canadian, Protestant European mixed-mutt from way back, plus a little Native American of the Mic-Mac tribe. If you saw me in the supermarket with my long hair up in a bun inspecting the ingredients on a can of vegetables, looking for the dreaded corn syrup, you might mistake me for a conservative librarian. But if you saw me on the dance floor at some hot salsa club in the city, or sneaking in a little nude sunbathing tucked away in some nook, you might think something else. Let's just say that my sense of curiosity and adventure runs the gamut! All right, now onto the church office interview story . . . My kids were finally in middle school, and I was looking for a mother's-hours job. Sporting a business degree and office experience, I took the normal route for a part-time office job and contacted a temporary placement agency. I went in and happily took all the computer tests. Great. Next stop was the face to face interview with the agent. In my hand during the interview was a copy of their local newspaper ad. Passing it across the table at the right moment, I indicated my interest in the part-time office/publishing job in the highly historic New Hampshire village center. As my finger pointed to the exact offering I was interested in, he stopped cold. He stared at me, and his eyes began to narrow; he was calculating something about me. Definitely sizing me up about something. I was a bit taken aback. Slowly he said one simple sentence: "This job is at a church."

Then it was my turn to stop and stare back. My eyebrows slightly rose as I pondered how this could be. Churches use temp agencies? What do they even do at a church office? I had no church experience on my resume. Hell, I hadn't even been to church since I was eleven. I was non-religious, to put it politely. In my busy adult life I never thought about religion at all. Confusion took a seat beside me at this interview, and I think I only managed to reply "Really?" through my stiff-lipped poker face. *Was* this a job I was interested in? I could NOT see myself as the proverbial "church secretary." Holy cow! He had to be kidding. I didn't even own any sensible shoes like the nuns wear. But I did have my hair twisted up into a tight bun, and was wearing a suit. The librarian side of me was at this interview, and the librarian vibe is a close cousin to the church secretary vibe.

"Does it matter what religion I am in order to get this job at the church?" I asked, rather awkwardly.

"As a matter of fact," he replied, "it would be illegal for them to ask what your religious affiliation is."

How very odd, wouldn't you say? What is this world coming to when a church can't even ask your religion when they are thinking of hiring you? I decided to go on the interview, because I liked the location in the beautiful village, and I like publishing. And because he told me the minister was a woman. Like Ginger Spice, I *love* girl-power. Yea, baby.

Long story short: I got the job, and I love it. I love the location, and the historic building. I love the parishioners, and the daily projects. I grew to really love the fact that I am able to have a positive impact on people nearly everyday. My job managing the church office has so many facets.

When the phone rings at my desk, it is like Forrest Gump's box of chocolates—you never know what you are gonna get. Funerals, weddings, baptisms, family reunions, donation calls, rental calls, suicide calls, sales calls, musicians or their agents, news editors, reporters from NPR, artists, authors, rabbis, priests, nuns, lesbians and gays, professors, scientists, Homeland Security, Fire Marshals, realtors, florists, caterers, accountants, contractors, doctors, lawyers, liars, volunteers, chefs, master gardeners, steeplejacks, genealogists, retired folks, overworked folks, unemployed folks, mentally disturbed folks, or even just the boss checking in. Yep, just like a box of chocolates!

Food Pantry

Part of the mission of the church that I work at is to help others in need, like Jesus did, regardless of their situation. To fulfill part of that mission, the church began a small food pantry a decade ago that has been steadily growing ever since. On Thursdays of each week, from ten in the morning to noon, the door is open and usually has about twenty-five visitors. I can see the folks lining up outside my window, rain or shine, waiting their turn to be admitted into the tiny building that houses the dry-goods pantry. Church volunteers run the project, and have gotten to know the regulars, as have I. The typical patrons can be divided into three main groupings: single mothers with young children, elderly on a fixed income, and employment-challenged males (disabled or addicted or just unlucky). In addition, the working poor have to come by every so often, especially around the holidays, to make ends meet. Here are three stories from the pantry.

The recession brought many newly unemployed men to the door, as the unemployment rate shot up to 10 percent. One Thursday, a recently unemployed man was apologizing profusely to me for having to use the pantry. I could feel my skin flush and my blood pressure rise. I was getting very angry at this poor man, but I didn't even know why. He was a pretty nice guy it seemed; after all he was showing a lot of sincere humility. This anger had bubbled up from my subconscious, and I wondered why. After he left my office, I put some serious energy into finding the root of this sudden mysterious anger. "All right, Marie, calm down and let's look at this together," I said out loud to myself. After some quiet, it dawned on me that I was angry because he said he felt embarrassed and horrified that he had to now get help from a pantry and other town services. "Really, Mr. Man?" I thought. Well, this is something that some single mothers have had to do for centuries, regardless of their horror, as if it were normal or expected or fair just because they are the gender with a womb. My childhood anger at having lived this came popping out. I remembered my mom working at crazy jobs at all hours, and all I could see was government cheese and revenge. Bam, it was such a strong emotion that gripped me! It came on like a rhino in full charge! Yikes! But then my enlightened light-being self just acknowledged that feeling, and let it pass. There will always be folks hungry and looking for free food. The good thing is, now that these formerly easily employable men have had to actually deign to get food from the pantry because of the recession, perhaps they will donate more when the job market returns to normal. Awareness is the first step. Blessings to you, Mr. Man.

Next story. Some folks who get suddenly down on their luck will drag around defeated and complaining forever more. I call them the drama kings and queens. You may know some. Others will rise to the challenge and make their lives better than ever, like Victoria. When Victoria called me one morning I thought she was a drama queen. Her story was wild and involved lack of shoes, no car, and an abusive husband just today hauled off by the police. I gave her the address of the pantry and told her to come whenever she could: I would unlock the door off-hours for her.

She got a ride from the cops and was dropped off within the hour. Wearing weird boots and sporting a huge purple eye like I had never seen before, she walked into my office. She looked eerily like my sister, and it freaked me out that this *could* be my sister, or anyone's sister, if the circumstances were just a little different. She rambled on and on about her situation. Her hated husband. Her autistic teen-aged daughter. She was definitely still traumatized and in shock. I think I was too. I have no training in social work, and luckily, no history of domestic violence.

I felt it in my heart for this sister goddess. I unlocked the door and gave her about three times the limit of food. That turned out to be the day that she finally admitted to herself that her husband was a bum, and she was not taking it anymore. She sent him to jail. She got on all the town services for this situation. She moved. She got a job. Her daughter joined Special Olympics and won medals. Her grades went way up in school, and she made a lot of friends. On the one year anniversary of the day I met her, she wrote an inspirational letter to the editor of the village newspaper. "All women who suffer in silence to speak up; People will believe you, people will help you." Yes, they will. Sister to sister, goddess to goddess.

And then there is Muriel. She is elderly, less than mobile, and can't make ends meet on her fixed income. Yet her white hair is always curled in the cutest coif, and her bright and clear blue eyes have a mischievous sparkle. Her mind is sharp and clever, and she can see the humor in nearly every situation. Between giggles she will tell you how, as a young girl, she used to work for a congressman in DC, but then gave it up when she married because wives didn't work then. Or how her husband turned out to be an abusive alcoholic and she had to go see the Catholic Cardinal and beg to get granted a divorce. Or how she then was a working single mom in the days when that wasn't hip (yes, she used the word "hip"). Or how she finally got remarried, but when her second husband got older, he got sick and died, and she lost everything, even the house, to his medical bills.

She calls me weekly from her tiny rented apartment to discuss what type of food I will pack for her food pantry bag. Bran muffins are her favorite, so if the local bakery sends over some day-olds I squirrel them away for her. Sometimes I will drop the weekly bag by her apartment, if she can't get the town helpers to pick it up. She shuffles slowly to the door with a big grin. That woman is such a spitfire: I am astounded.

Muriel, like a sprite, laughs everyday. Always a joke, a compliment, or something funny in the news or on TV to tell me about. Never a bad word about anything. She is a wise crone-goddess: happy and at peace with what she has. Alive and vibrant, she still looks forward to every single day. I am blessed by you, old Crone divine.

These three people have taught me lessons, changed my views, and have affected me profoundly. What luck! My job—helping others in the way of Jesus—teaches me great lessons in compassion and humility in the face of humanity.

The Search for Spirituality Begins

In my third year of employment at the church, slowly I began to shift away from being non-religious. This is where the tale really begins. Hold your torch a bit higher, and don't let your hair catch on fire.

Being goal-oriented, I make New Year's resolutions. I resolved to "explore my spirituality." Each December I give some thought to where I want to head in the New Year. Sometimes I set a concrete goal such as learning to speak Italian. Sometimes I just have a vague feeling. This was one of those years. Notice the verb: Explore.

Every Monday morning, part of my routine was to go into the church building proper, and take a look around. I collect names from the visitor log, throw away random trash, straighten out hymnals, nametags, brochures, whatever, look for leftover food or cookies (yum), put the chairs back in order, turn off any forgotten lights, and take the leftover floral arrangements to my desk. (Flowers are my number one favorite perk of the job.)

During my third year, something changed. I became aware of the "holy vibe." The church sanctuary is very old, so I am talking the holy vibe of 200 plus years running. Often, while approaching the stern and steadfast communion table in front of the pulpit on my weekly flower raid, I would stop and sit quietly in the front pew and try hard to soak up the holy vibe. I often would randomly open the Bible to where it fell, and see if the passage spoke to me. It never really did. I often listened for ghosts, or echoes of voices past, or even mice. I never heard any. I often stood at the front up on the stage, behind the pulpit podium, to see if a light from heaven would shine down and enlighten me because I was standing in a powerful spot. I remained in the questioning darkness.

From up in the pulpit one can look out across the pews, or into the choir loft, or towards the sound booth, and notice what is happening at all the entrances and exits. This is a great vantage point from which to run the show. When you get to understand how something really works, it can lose its magic. You know what I mean? I could see how the Wizard of Oz could operate this old sanctuary manually. No disembodied holy light shines down on the pulpit from the mighty heavens. It is human inspiration and perspiration that runs the worship each Sunday.

While seated in the pews I began to notice something. When randomly opening the Bible for a verse that might inspire, words like "enemy" or "smite" came up too often for my taste. I prefer not to surround myself with negative thoughts, so I couldn't "hear" the Bible, even in that holy space. I would rather look to the lilies, and listen to them.

All right, hold your torch lower just now, and shine some light down here in the pew for a minute. As I sat silently, all alone in a sanctuary that could seat 400 comfortably, what began to happen is this. Slowly, over the months, I began to "hear" what was inside of me. What luck! Yes, inside me. That is where you should look, too. It is so simple it's crazy.

This is how it happened. I tagged along on a confirmation class church field trip on comparative religion to a Buddhist retreat center, and I got the tour. In the meditation room, we sat for a half hour of silence and incense. I loved the incense. Very funky. It was then that I got the first inkling that the divine may be inside of me, instead of on the outside where I had been previously searching for it. I wanted to try it again. I wanted to hone this internal listening skill. Shortly after the church field trip, I returned to the Buddhist center with my kids and my sister. We all went to participate in the hour-long New Year's Day Meditation Marathon for World Peace. Totally fascinating. Incense, pillows, blue-faced statues. And an hour-long silence. Forty people sitting silently together in various forms of lotus positions or mudras. I found it intensely peaceful. My kids found it intensely painful to sit silently for that long. Teenagers, go figure.

When the meditation gong sounded, signaling the end, we all stretched. The man beside me let out his breath in several long, loud Lion's Breaths, which is a very intense form of eliminating all the old air from your lungs, causing him to make the craziest prolonged grimace my kids had ever seen on the face of a full-grown man. Their eyes widened as they tried not to stare impolitely. They giggled all the way to the car, and commented to me that they thought he was deranged or something.

Admittedly, he did look like a Chinese dragon in the particular way his eyes bulged out and his lips stretched way back, showing all his teeth! I could not convince my kids that he was normal. I still chuckle about that when I do a Lion's Breath myself.

After that, I decided to research Buddhism to see if it was the thing I had been looking for. Turns out that it was not. But it did introduce me to silence, breathing, Chi (or life force/energy), and a love of incense.

Back in the pews. On Monday mornings I would try to meditate in the Buddhist fashion. But it never went too well. Perhaps because I was fitting my meditation into the ten-minute time slot I had before I needed to get back to work. Later, I did better.

Good Vibrations

On the warm, sunny days of that spring I ended my working day in mid-afternoon. Then, I would journey up, up, up, and up again, into the historic bell tower that once housed a Paul Revere bell. What a gorgeous view! It is the highest spot of the village center. Looking to the east past the bustling avenues, I was greeted with a panorama of trees, rolling hills, and a curly blue ribbon of a tidal river dancing through it all. Looking to the west, I was presented with a crow's nest view of a very old prep school campus. Classic red brick with old chimneys sprouting up like mushrooms everywhere. To the south is the roof of the post office . Ugly, take my word for it.

Ah! But looking to the north I saw only sky. There I could meditate. Big blue sky. No distractions. Simply sky. Sky and breath. No thoughts. No thinking. Monkey-mind be gone! If a thought comes, say hello and goodbye to it in the same breath and let it fly away into the blue. Close your eyes and let yourself fly away into the warm sun on your face.

Breath. Sky.

Breath. Sky.

Breath. Sky. Peace.

Breath. Sun. Peace.

Breath. Joy. Sun. Smile.

It is just as simple as that. Really, I am not kidding. Really. It is orgasmagical.

Clearing my head, heart, and lungs brings me to simplicity and silence. Simplicity and silence expand my internal vibration and bring me to a peaceful place. The divine intuition can then be heard. What luck!

You may have noticed the "internal vibration" I casually mentioned. What is that? I am not a scientist, but let me state some facts about "Inner Space." All matter is comprised of molecules. All molecules are made up of atoms. All atoms have various electrons in orbit around the nucleus. These moving electrons cause the whole atom to "vibrate." Different types vibrate at different speeds. What makes the electrons move/vibrate? No one knows, not even the quantum physicists. Now, there is something to really splash your torch light over and consider.

Consider this also: the classic case of various vibrational speeds on a molecule of water (H_2O). Coldness slows the vibration. Therefore, water that is in a very cold environment slows down its vibration until it turns to its denser form: ice. Water that is in a very hot environment speeds up, racing faster and faster until it turns to its lightest form: steam. In some bizarre twist, could the same forces be at work in the human experience?

Rocks are vibrating very slowly. A garden herb is vibrating more quickly. A human is somewhere in the middle, at about 60 MHz. Interesting, eh? Furthermore, if you the human, eat the herb, you increase your vibration for a while before you shift back to your baseline. You can actually incur a shift in your baseline by eating unprocessed foods and herbs.

Now, the point of increasing your chi, or vibration, is to get back to or rediscover your true self, your simple self. When you find your true and simple self, everything moves with the flow, and struggles, angst, stress, sickness, and all that other yucky stuff lessens, then eventually ceases. Life becomes a joy and the universe conspires to assist you in bliss. Everything goes Zen. I swear it.

The Goddess Deck

Now, remember, it was my New Year's resolution that year to "explore my spirituality." My huckleberry boyfriend Jake and I were over at his sister Eileen's house one day and I saw that Eileen had a few books on spirituality. We chatted a little about the topic, and then she offered to do a reading for me with some cards. Those funny little tarot cards that contain the dreaded "death card" are what I thought she was talking about. I had seen them in the movies, and thought they had more to do with magic than religion. Turns out, they have to do with neither. They have to do with spirituality. What luck!

Eileen got out her deck of cards, beautifully slick and gilded. That was the first time I laid eyes on the goddess deck, and they spoke to me. If the voice of the deck could have been heard, I am sure it would have lilted out the tune "O, sweet mystery of life at last I've found you . . ." The gold gilding on the edge of the deck gleamed at me and winked.

Jake and I sat across from his sister at the dining table. Eileen had me shuffle the cards, in order to imbue them with my chi or something. The glossy deck had a certain weight in my hands. I was told to pick three cards and place them face down in front of her. She said this would represent my past, present, and future. What drama! We all leaned in.

The first card, my past, showed Vesta, Roman goddess of home and hearth. Yes, that is what I had been when I was a stay-at-home mom for the past seventeen years. Domestic goddess for sure! Next, Diana, Roman moon goddess displayed the phrase "focused intention" on her card. My current reality at that time was that of an aging stay-at-home mom turned grad-student, with my eye on the target of a master's degree in business communications. Yes, that card made perfect sense to me as well. Freaky. Maybe there was something to this card thing?

Now was the big one. Now was what would be my future. What would it be? I had not the foggiest idea. Do you have any idea where you are headed? Those in the dark will say no. Those with a goddess torch might say yes at some point. Those in the light will just smile, even before you ask the question, because they are there already.

13

I had no idea where I was going to at the time. I felt as if I were completely in a dark and blinding snowstorm, being pulled along by a dog sled to some unknown destination. The dog-sled was my pursuit of the master's degree. I didn't know where it would lead me, but I hoped it would take me somewhere safe and comfortable. Maybe it was the vehicle, maybe it wasn't. Was it taking me to my future?

The card was turned over to reveal Sarasvati, Hindu goddess of the Arts. We all laughed. Here I was, seated next to my boyfriend who held a bachelors in Fine Arts, being told he was my future. How's that for confirmation of a fairly new relationship? But was that all, a future controlled outside myself in the form of my mate? Possibly this Arts card was revealing a glimpse of something else in the arts as well. This book perhaps? Hmmm. Immediately falling in love with the cards, I made a mental note to purchase my own deck at some point.

Many months later while attending a breathing workshop at a beautiful holistic center, I did finally see the goddess deck on a display shelf, its golden box shining bright. "O sweet mystery of life, at last I've found you . . ." began playing in my head as I joyously whipped out my credit card. Cha-ching! I brought those forty-four goddesses home, and they have been inspiring me ever since. What luck! Actually, anytime I sprinkle in the phrase "what luck" while telling you my story, what it actually means is that something that was supposed to happen has happened. Destiny manifesting. Get it?

Do you believe in Destiny? What about Free Will? What about Dr. Carl Jung's "Synchronicity?" Read on. Perhaps this book is in your hands right now for a reason. What luck for you! Come on, say it out loud finally: WHAT LUCK! It is time for you to get Boom shaka-lucky too. I want to take you higher. Here we go!

Introducing the Goddesses of New Hampshire

I am fortunate to have a lot of women friends now. You might even say lucky. Wink. (Does one make their own luck?) I never realized before how important it is to have many friends. Each of these friends represents a different aspect of my personality. Some like the woods or the beach; some like to dance or cook; some like to do arts and crafts; some drink alcohol, and some do not; some are single; some are in relationships; but we are all on a spiritual journey together.

When spending time with these women individually at the beginning, at some point the talk would turn to men. I began to ponder if I should introduce them all to each other, since most at least had the topics of man-hunting and spirituality in common. Or would it turn out horribly, like the famous Jerry Seinfeld episode where George Costanza's "two worlds collide" with disastrous effects? Should I keep the good thing I have going as-is, or should I take a risk and introduce them all to each other. Hmmm.

The risk was taken.

All my new friends were invited to my new condo one cold evening, as winter was on the wane. Over candles and jazz, bruschetta and beer, they all faced each other around my large dining room table. Introductions were made, and the conversation flowed smoothly. People talked about themselves, and asked questions of others. There was a lot of laughter and introspection, as these powerful women all recognized the same energy in each other.

It was as if they each gave themselves as a gift to one another. Magic was in the air. All these strong women seated around the table fed power to each other. It was the inception of "the goddesses," and I could feel it. We vowed to create a group email list entitled "Sisterhood of the Traveling Pantyhose" and try to meet at least once a month. When I was once again alone in my condo, it gave me a glow to realize that my risk of introducing all my random new friends had really paid off. Exponentially. What luck!

Near Earth Day, we met again at another location to attend open studios to view Mother Earth exhibits. The air was warm, so we sat leisurely, post-exhibit, on a riverside porch. Via email I had informed the group that I would bring along my goddess deck. Most of them were not familiar with these cards. Those were the pre-goddess days.

When I first announced that it was my intention to bring the cards, I didn't know quite what would happen or why I even felt compelled to bring the deck. But I brought it. As we sat around that table in the spring air, it came to me not to do the traditional full three-card reading, but to just pass out one card to each friend. I did not know why, I just trusted my intuition. So I shuffled the deck for a while, then stopped. I presented each woman with her card, face down.

Turns out these random cards revealed our goddess personas to us. I guess that is what was meant to be. Sometimes the cards just guide you, as if you are simply a conduit through which they speak. Developing your intuition is one outcome of using cards on a regular basis.

The way the cards fell was most fitting. My good friend, the tall and graceful ballroom dancer of German/Polish descent, and mother of five children, was bestowed with Freya, the Nordic goddess of fertility and celebration. My other good friend, the Healing Arts Practitioner, drew Kali, Hindu goddess of endings and beginnings. My new artist friend, into the environment and having Native American roots, was honored with the card of Ixchel, Medicine Woman. My destiny fell to Aphrodite, the Greek goddess of love. How Boom shaka-lucky for this Scorpio woman! (This card also urged me to stand more in my feminine power.) Other goddesses in attendance included: Maeve, Sedna, Lakshimi, and Isolt. Only Isolt was not agreed upon, (you can't win them all!) so it was a good round for the most part.

Now, goddesses may seem like a frivolous and ancient word to use, but if you really think about it in an everyday modern fashion, it makes the utmost sense. It's primal. It's the way cultures began prior to the Garden of Eden story. Ask the Native Americans. Ask the Hindus who still live in the cradle of civilization. Ponder it for a minute, and then just relax into it. It's fun! You, dear reader, are a goddess too (or perhaps a god). It really is so simple; everyone has something that they are especially good at, or something they are drawn to or embody. What is it that is at your core? Perhaps a quick search on the internet will enable you to buy Doreen Virtue's Goddess Oracle Cards, and use your torch to spangle some enlightenment in your world. Make your own luck . . .

Back to the tale! The group of newly named goddesses then commenced with the frozen margaritas to discuss the luck of the draw and other matters. Other matters included mostly men. Men—where are they? How can you cull out a good one on Match.com and the like? And actually, who says there are any good ones? Call me a romanticist, but I say there are still some good ones out there. Take Jake. No, you can't—he's mine and I love him madly. I met Jake shortly after my marriage of eighteen years ended. After a few months of dating men wildly and sowing my Scorpion oats, there he appeared beside me one night. I liked the shape of his wrists, and his dark curly hair. Within one minute of talking, I knew there was some potential for further discussion there.

Funny how when it comes, it comes, and you damn well know it. There is a certain look in the eye, a thickness to the air. When two energies on the same wavelength meet, you can instantly feel it and the earth moves.

The Journey to Jake

At a random meeting at a pizza joint, he passed me his business card; an offer to start the dance. I accepted the card, looked at the name of his sculpture studio; drew my breath and readied my frame for the tango. An artist? Hot damn! I never met a real live hep-cat artist from the big city before. What an air of coolness he exuded. Very exotic yet humble, yes quite enticing. Hmmm, I think I will check out his Web site . . .

The first few steps of the ancient dance of woo came the next week when an invitation was extended for a personal studio tour at sunset. A lovely evening full of mutual interests, wine, and laughter; the dance had begun in full swing. From my perch in the Eames chair in the salon section of the studio, I could see the sun sinking into a colorful and romantic display through the enormous mill windows. After dark I tried to teach him the basic steps of several ballroom classics. He had on these groovy shoes that could kill a cockroach in a corner from the middle of the room. I was scared for my toes. We just ended up laughing, and agreeing to try again later as things went along. He walked me to my car and gave me the most soulful and sexy kiss I ever had. Even now, as I think about it, I begin to sizzle again.

After four years we are still sizzling and dancing and laughing and enjoying mutual interests. Jake is such an enlightened and simple soul. It turns out that he is a god of love as well. A nice match for Aphrodite. What luck! Sure, we have had our ups and downs, but what relationship has not? Together, afoot and light-hearted on the long brown path, we grow. As the poet Whitman once said: "He gives me his love, more precious than money, he gives himself to me before preaching or law. We shall scatter with lavish hand all that we earn or achieve." Walt nailed that one!

Jake and I hold each other dear, not too tight to choke, but not too loose to let the other down. We see ourselves in each other. He is part me, and I am part him, and will be forevermore, come what may. We both know it. He is a magical being, just like me. He is the yin to my yang, or put more correctly, the yang to my yin. The man is in touch with his feminine side, while still reeking of Jack Kerouac abandon.

During the times when I slip, and am walking around in a state of refried confusion, he is my rock and pulls me out of the pit. During the regular, work-a-day, comfortable times, his fascinating mind always delights and surprises me. And even during those special times when I am floating around in blossoms of joy, he can further set my petals all a-flutter, so that we may float even higher towards the sun. For he is the captain of romance. He is my huckleberry friend, and we are both looking for the same rainbow's end.

I wonder what card the universe would bestow him with, were I to draw one for him? (I think I will never draw a goddess personae card for a male. It is just not right! Heaven forbid I should mess up his mojo.)

First Crack in the Cosmic Egg

Let me tell you, things were not always bopping along magically like this, as you may have discerned from the casual mention of my eighteen-year marriage.

I was the typical suburban housewife, and didn't I have it all? Husband with big job, two beautiful daughters, colonial in the executive neighborhood, Southern vacation home on the gated golf course, new cars, big-screen TVs, and all the latest gadgets. I was the dedicated wife and mother, the PTA president, the volunteer to all good causes. Our family was even picked from a crowd at Disney World as the sample happy family to light the Christmas tree one night. Alas! The façade that is Disney was also the façade that was my loveless marriage. We both knew it, but struggled on for the sake of the girls. I slept in my own bedroom for the final seven years of our marriage. I am sure you can name a few of your friends living the same lie. I smashed it down so deep inside me that it became officially repressed for years.

The spring solstice brought it bubbling to the surface in that eighteenth year. Events that I once thought were random, I now believe are synchronistic: a funny and easy way of saying that the universe is conspiring for your happiness. Being a New England winter-loather I have always been joyous when spring comes to finally shoo winter out the back door. So, that particular year some odd solstice celebration thingy, having something to do with crystals or something, caught my eye. Yes, I could do that for my boring scheduled once-a-season-night-out-for-fun.

It seemed it could be fun and adventurous to go look at some shiny baubles and drink some wine with my sister and aunt in celebration of the coming of spring. I went in blind, and came out initiated to spirituality. Only I didn't know it then. I didn't know quite what had happened that night, just that it scared me a little it was so strong. The great spiritual writer Henri Nouwen wrote " all momentous occasions are unnoticed until they pass by." Now ain't that the truth?

Alrighty, bear down your torch on this small sparkly blue gem. Look sharp. To continue the tale: I am waiting for my turn as the crystal reader starts explaining to the women in the circle, one by one, what the crystal or stone means that they chose from the pile. I am watching very intently, as this is very interesting. Interesting in the way you might watch a National Geographic documentary about strange peoples far away. You are unattached emotionally, just curiously watching it play out, and as soon as it is over you will click off the channel, unaffected, and go unload the dishwasher or something. There I sat with my shiny, translucent, aquamarine placed in front of me.

She came around to me and told me the aquamarine represents the throat chakra. What the heck is a chakra? She explained that the crystal indicates that I need to pay attention to my throat energy. To speak my true thoughts; just let them rip. To stop taking everything dumped on you and stand up for yourself. To use my voice.

Hmm, use my voice? Did I have one, and if I did, what did I possibly have to say? My mind was blank.

I was a fairly happy person and life was going along OK. Or so I was trying oh so very hard to convince myself. What if what I said would rock the proverbial boat? Oh no, I couldn't even think a thought at that moment that would rock the boat. Because, as I mentioned, I was repressed and didn't even know it. So, I took in what she had to say, filed it under, "I wonder what that odd comment is all about," and she went on to the next person. And the next and next. Then she got to the last woman, who had a rose quartz heart waiting in front of her.

"The rose quartz symbolizes gentle love. This stone is saying to you that you need to find a fulfilling love in your life, it is extremely important, and it can be either romantic or platonic," the crystal reader began her explanation. I cocked my head in interest, as I had with all the previous explanations. Suddenly, out of nowhere I was filled with such a rush of emotion that I could not breathe and I almost choked out loud. I was taken by such surprise that my head split in half. Out popped a devil and an angel, and they took up their positions on opposite shoulders. I remained a stunned and silent observer in the middle. Nobody else in the room noticed this spectacle.

"It is true, it is all true," stated the fluffy pink angel, nonchalantly.

"What a load of crap," retorted the red devil.

Still stunned, I wondered what they were talking about, and how it pertained to me. My eyes burned. I struggled to hold back the tears, so as to not look like a fool in the room full of people. I think I even let out a little gasp, in an effort to gain control of myself. I had no idea why I was crying. The two floaters–pink and red—paid no attention to me whatsoever as their conversation went on.

The devil creature swathed in a red BBQ apron festooned with PTA pins continued "Love is bullshit, and it is not gonna pay the bills. Love dies, but responsibilities never die. The minute you became a wife and mother, you forfeited yourself for eternity. You forfeited love, and replaced it with security, schedules, and swimming pools. Your proper name got scratched from the books and replaced with the nouns *wife* and *mother*, like a million other nameless women. Suck it up, sister. No love for you. Life ain't a fairy-tale. End of story."

The red demon had a logical argument. I was in full agreement with her view.

After an amused pause, the rebuttal came from the pink luminous one. "Silly little red fool, why do you limit her? This little merry-go-round she is on is not all there is. She can step off it at any time. She has always had the power to do this." And then she smiled beatifically, flicked her wand, and made a small and sparkling rose quartz pendant appear around my neck.

Poof, they were both gone and I was left looking around the room, amazed at what had just happened. My eyes darted back and forth as I scanned the room to see if anyone had noticed me squirming with my glossy eyes bulging out. Nobody had. Good. The readings had finished and it was now being announced that we could all help ourselves to the refreshments. After a minute or two of being forced to mingle (while in this stupor), I was free to leave the workshop. In the parking lot I asked my sister and aunt if they felt anything weird happen that night. They said no. So I didn't say anything either. I didn't want to be like the one who says they saw a UFO, and get labeled cuckoo.

Apparently, this angel/devil argument is what I had to say, and since I couldn't admit it to myself, my mind, or the aquamarine, or the universe, shoved it down my throat in a singular flash of ugly insight.

I was so thankful when I finally got to be alone, after this sudden and strong insight, which seemed to come from both inside, and *outside* of me at the same time. Odd. Very odd. And then I got a little scared. I was cracking up, there was no doubt about it. Yep. I was losing it. What the heck just happened back there? I had never experienced anything as suddenly surprising and ugly like that before. Ok, well if you don't count the time in high school that I had that boil on my face from the Royal Jelly Bee Cream (I am allergic—who knew?). After staying out of school for two days, the thing finally burst by accident when I was washing my face in the mirror one morning half asleep. Raising my face up from the wash basin, I took the steaming wash cloth away from my face and saw a fistful of green goo sliding down my cheek. It took me by surprise and it hurt like the dickens when the goo burst through the skin and started drooling. I didn't realize so much goo could be packed in one human cheek. Packed in, smashed down, repressed. Explosive. Just like tonight.

Looking back now at the solstice crystal night, I can see it was the first crack in my cosmic eggshell. The first message the universe sent me was: use your voice, stop being a doormat, you deserve a loving relationship and you have the power to make this happen. Well, maybe it was not the first message the universe sent me, but it was damn well the first one I actually noticed. It took me about a month to decipher this, and make some vague plans. I left my loveless house soon thereafter. With my imaginary rose quartz pendant dangling at my breast, I leapt and waited for the net to appear.

Dear reader, I now invite you to stop, and reflect, on how your own circumstances relate to my tales. The fun and enlightening TORCH TIME activities are placed throughout the book to assist you. In addition, I will introduce you to a goddess from the golden deck of cards. Meditate on the essence of this goddess, within yourself, to help guide you in that area of your reflection. Here now I serve you your first food for thought. Flambé style!

♦ Torch Time 1 ♦

Shine the light of your torch this way. See if you can't get some light to fall on something you have hidden away in the dark corners of your mind by just blurting out the first thing that comes to mind when I ask the following questions.

Meet the goddess: Pele is the Hawaiian goddess of volcanoes. Let your divine passion erupt, and be honest with yourself. What is your heart's true desire? Take baby steps towards it.

1. If an angel and a devil right now suddenly appeared on your two shoulders, what topic(s) would they be bickering about?

_____

_____

_____

_____

What would the devil say? _____

_____

_____

_____

_____

What would the angel dreamily reply? _____

_____

_____

_____

_____

2. Write down three small steps your inner goddess would take to help the angel win: _____

_____

_____

_____

_____

The seeds are now planted. Water them and give them light, then watch them erupt!

The Bottomless Abyss

I knew divorce would be hard, but I was determined, and blissfully ignorant. I arrived one rainy spring night at my sister's doorstep with some of my clothes in a hefty garbage bag. Classic. I moved into the bottom of her split ranch in the village on a street named Haven Lane. Seriously, does it get more synchronistic than that? I read books about divorce, a lot of books. (Did I mention I was voted the Class Bookworm in eighth grade?) The books all said the same thing: it takes an average of three years to rebound from a divorce and feel that life is "normal" again. Ha! I was strong and I had a plan, it would be all straightened out in one year or less. Period. However, in the meantime these series of unfortunate events occurred:

May—it was the rainiest, grayest May in history with forty days straight of rain bringing flood levels to New Hampshire not seen in one-hundred years. Depressing.

Beginning of June—my two best forever-single friends flat out dumped me. Both suddenly marrying and living happily ever after. Wonderful for them. Depressing for me.

End of June—my lifelong friend of forty years, who had been battling cancer for two years, took a big turn for the worse and suddenly died. So frigging depressing.

Beginning of July—my oldest daughter got her driver's license, and the empty nest syndrome took its first menacing step toward me, as she and her sister jumped in the car and sped away while I choked on their road dust. Maternally depressing.

End of July—Real estate bubble burst and market began a downhill slide that was to last for years. The Southern vacation properties I needed to sell, so I could buy my own New Hampshire condo, hemorrhaged value. This did not leave me enough money to buy a condo. Tip: Beware of bad and lazy divorce lawyers! Financially depressing.

By August I was beat. I was so damn depressed that I cried multiple times every day. I read that divorce and death are the top two stressors. I had gotten the double-whammy. And some extra bonuses besides. What luck!

What luck?? Why do I say "what luck" right here, at this point in the story when my life is such a big bowl of ugly? "C'mon, you've got to be joking," is what you are thinking, right? Well, there is truth to the old cowboy saying "that which doesn't kill you makes you stronger." I had leapt, sure there would be a net. Instead I was falling down and down, and down some more. It was an abyss! What a learning experience those months were. Finally, the net kicked in at the start of fall. I had enrolled in grad school and dance lessons, in the early winter I met Jake, and in the early spring I met Faith (otherwise known as Kali, Hindu goddess of endings and beginnings).

Endings, Beginnings

That spring I was coming to the end of my two-year commitment for the high school PTA. Because of the divorce, I didn't even live in the school district for the entire final year. Dang! But I finished out my term like a good girl. One of my last projects was a comedy show fundraiser, for which I was listed as the contact to purchase tickets. A woman contacted me by email, and her address was local in the village, so I invited her to come on by my office at the church to pick them up. The next day I looked up from my desk to see a woman coming through the door. Her shoulder-length hair was sandy blond and fluffy like Farrah Fawcett, minus the flip. It flowed and glowed against the yellow walls of my office as she approached me. Energy and light filled the room in such a way that I became energized myself. And that is how I met Faith. Her energy was my exact wavelength, and she had me at Hello.

At a fancy tea shop a few days later, we traded life stories over hot pots of tea. She was a massage therapist who also did Rieki at her studio. Like me, she was divorced and had two teen girls, and lived downtown in the village. She was on my same path, but much further along. Her torch was shining so bright I needed sunglasses!

Look at her, I thought. *She has made a real life of her own. She stands solidly in her feminine power. She supports herself, takes orders from no Mr. Man, and is happy, healthy, and wise with a big circle of happy and healthy friends.* I told her of my grandiose plans to finish grad school and get a big fancy job in pharmaceuticals to support myself. I needed to get this killer job, I told her, so that I could move out of my sister's basement and buy my own condo. She just smiled. She told me that she often saw herself as a bridge; she takes people from one ending to a new beginning. She was very spiritual. I had never met anyone like her. I can see now in hindsight, that her goddess essence pulled mine out of the woods and onto the long brown path, that day in the tea shop. She shared the flame of her already blazing torch, and ignited mine, which I didn't even know I had with me. (I am forever grateful to you, sister goddess.) After the teapots were empty, we then made plans to go to a village bar and dance the following week. Ok, so you can't be spiritual all the time!

Three years later, (yes, the exact timing all the divorce books said) I, Marie, am now empowered with the essence of Aphrodite, goddess of love, and my torch blazes brightly. I have love and respect, that starts within myself. I stand solid in my feminine power now. What luck! Where does this luck come from? Shh, it's a secret: The Universe conspires to give you what you want. Chuckle if you want, but you know that you at least hope it is true! The tricky part is to know what you want: what is for your highest good? If you need a clue about this, I suggest you check into Mike Dooley's book *Infinite Possibilities* and see what you can see, about how to make your own lucky magic.

Full Moon Meditation

After a while of hanging out with Faith and having various conversations about my fledgling spirituality, she invited me to her meditation group. The group was held monthly near the full moon, at an old farmhouse over the state line. It was to be a guided meditation spoken by an enlightened woman, Natalie, who was channeling angelic messages. I had no idea what to expect. The people in attendance were shamans, reiki practitioners, spiritual counselors, other highly enlightened persons, and me. I just kept my mouth shut and my eyes open. Soft music played in the background, while Natalie's gentle and whispery voice took us on a journey that began in the candle-lit room. Hanging in the air was the smell of burning sage. Eyes closed, I drifted into a lovely meditation that was so relaxing and peaceful.

No, I did not hear any angelic voices in my head. No, I did not catch a glimpse of any auras. I got no messages from the "other side." Expectations like that were probably the result of watching too much TV! What I did get was a profound sense of peace, and a noticeable expansion of my joy and energy vibration. A prayer for world peace concluded that segment of the marvelous evening. This was followed by a flurry of activity and chatter as we left the shadowy room and moved into the bright kitchen.

The evening was free, but the requested donation was either food, money, or candles. Food always wins. The group bellied up to the loaded farmhouse table and discussed impressions and emotions evoked during the meditation. They updated each other on their lives since last month. It was a joyous din. I enjoyed the meditation so much that I became a regular member. Watching the moon wax each month brings a smile to my face and joy to my heart. Full moon meditation draws near. What an adventurous journey, a wonderful new beginning, courtesy of Kali: the goddess of endings and beginnings, and Faith too!

The New Earth

As I began to understand that life should not be a struggle, and that actually it should be a daily joy, (which it was becoming) I began to wonder what it was that I was put here on earth to do. What to do? What to do? What to do for a job? Is that the real question? I thought it might be. Or maybe it was something else. I was stumped.

In order to try to figure it out I did what I always do: I hit the books. What a plethora of literature in the new age section of the village library. I read and I read and I read. (Don't forget, I was the class bookworm back in the day. I can read like lightning!) I read as much as I could. I pondered on the local stone labyrinth path. I don't watch TV anymore, so I have all that couch time free. I got through all the good books at the library, but there was one that eluded me. I had my name on the waiting list, and it was not coming anytime soon, as I was about the twentieth on the list.

So I ordered it on the internet and look! it was an Oprah book club selection and I got such a deal! However, I had only read one other Oprah selection, and I had to put it down in horror and dismay—something I rarely do, being a bibliophile. It wasn't my favorite genre, but it was written by a local author over the state line, so I thought I would give it a whirl a couple of years ago when it came out and a friend passed it to on me. It was a dark story about a house in dispute, and its tragedy upon sandy tragedy greatly saddened me. What a drag. I was hoping this book I had just ordered would not suck me down as well.

The book came lickity-split, and I settled onto my new red microfiber sofa in my sister's cellar to read about what would be my purpose in life. Would it magically tell me something about what kind of job I should pursue? Thank God! Please! Somebody tell me what I should be doing and put me out of this continued state of confusion!

Well, it didn't tell me what to do for a job. Not really. It went way beyond that. The job is just a means to an end. The "end" is what you should be doing. The journey is actually the "end" if there is any "end" to be had past the Now. What kind of life one should pursue would be a better description of the tome. It was so interesting that it took me a long time to read it, because I had to keep stopping to ponder the deepness of nearly every idea presented. I digested small chunks of it over a couple of days and nights. One night, as I reclined on the red sofa pushed up against the yellow walls, I began to read the chapter on Inner Space.

Mr. Tolle began to explain how inner space is even vaster than outer space. Imagine the distance between the sun and Jupiter, and then multiply that by one hundred. Imagine that great distance, and then shrink the scale to fit the atoms and the orbiting neutrons in the cells in your body. That is how much space is in you. You are basically vibrating air/space! As is the sofa I was on, the house I was in, the entire village, and the elements in the atmosphere I was breathing at that moment. Wow! I had not understood that fully before. Stunned, I rested the book on my lap and closed my eyes to thoughtfully consider the wonder of this amazing fact. And then . . .

Boom! A veil was whipped off my eyes. White blackness closed in from the sides of my vision at an incredibly rapid speed, as my awareness expanded and exploded in the opposite direction at the same rate of speed. In less than an instant I was at one with the universe . . . no, actually I had the feeling that I was the universe. I was total awareness in space. I was no longer on the sofa, but in the blackness and brightness of outer space, floating among the stars. Or possibly inner space, floating as the void between the objects? Or maybe I was a star too? I had no limit or boundary, and I clearly felt that. I was the space. This all happened so suddenly that if I were standing up I would have fallen down. Yet, strangely, it was profoundly peaceful. This instant took my breath away and made me dizzy from the release of physical laws. Blissfully, I basked in the awareness and peace . . .

. . . For only about three seconds. Then the monkey in my mind finally came out of its shock and started a quiet nervous chatter: "Oh my God! Where are we?" I heard it say. It, not me. I was unbounded space and energy. My observation shifted towards the monkey, and the universe zipped itself up away from me. Literally. Blinding white and blinding black flashes. It made me dizzy once again. I fought to ignore the monkey mind, as I suddenly understood the chatter was losing me this sacred glimpse. I was successful. I was flashed back into the peace and floating once again. But only for a second, or not even. Dang! I had lost it again. The monkey was scared and came back ferociously screaming SHIT! WHAT THE HELL IS THIS? WHERE ARE WE?!!

And then it was all gone, and I realized I was back in the room and stuck by gravity on the sofa. I had a distinct feeling of gravity weighing down my body into the couch again.

I would have loved to have seen the look on my face at that exact moment. Amazed? Stunned? Speechless? Beyond that, way beyond that. Probably more like the face of someone in shock who had just shit their pants. I am sure that when Siddhartha disappeared into the atmosphere as he sat by the river, he was infinitely more graceful about it.

I was so scared and confused that it took me almost a year before I ever mentioned it to anyone. The words that I have chosen to share this with you in this book do not come even close to really describing the experience. Sorry. Truly. I hope you get to see this for yourself one day, and if you have already, that my description helps you to feel the leftover resonance of yours. If all beings had this mystical experience, even once, the world would be a better place.

Now, instead of being apprehensive about this experience, I consider it a blessing, another crack in the cosmic eggshell, more flame to my torch. Thanks, Mr. Tolle. At first I thought that your New Earth book didn't reveal my life's purpose to me. It took me a while to figure out what happened there on the couch. But now I get it. Thank you! Grateful beyond words is how I feel about having been given this extraordinary gift of total awareness, total divine energy, blinding light, through an out-of-body-experience. I can't even imagine anything more lucky than that! Baby, baby, baby, light my fire. Boom shaka-laka-lucky. Boom! Boom!

Respect the Pie

Well, that was quite the spiritual experience. But I would not call it religious. Religion seems such an outdated word to me, full of dogma and rules. Religion is like a pie, and true spirituality/love is the sacred space in the center of the pie. That is my philosophy.

You don't understand? Well, let me expand! Simply put, imagine a pie cut into pieces and still warm in the baking dish. The many, many slices represent Christianity, Judaism, Islam, Hinduism, Buddhism, Confucianism, Native American Spiritualism, Wicca, and etc., ad infin. Then there are the folks who find it on their own through Perennialism, or a twelve-step program like AA or by having a near death experience, or maybe a freaky out-of-body-experience. They are all slices too. And let us not forget the fence-sitters who say, "I don't know what it is, but there is something out there." They are a slice too, as undefined as they are. At the very center of the pie, all the pieces touch. That is the sameness. Right where the pieces touch, this is what they all have in common. What is the common factor?

Recognition of a benevolent creative force.

In other words: recognition of Love/Energy. This benevolent creative force is all you need. It goes by many names: God, Allah, Buddha, Awareness, Spirit, Magic, "Something out there," etc. Forget about all the other tasty and various pieces of the pie with their singular crusts. The crusty ends can get caught up in dogma, discrimination, arguments and wars. At the very center, at the warm core, all slices aim at the same thing, they all meld into one. They all come from the same place. Love is the center. Why not skip the human imposed dogma, and the various holy texts and names, and get right to the heart of it?

Respect the Benevolent-Creative-Force pie, but stay away from the crusty edges and head for the softly vibrating center. Each slice of pie is a different path to walk to arrive at the same spiritual destination. None is the only way, none is the wrong way. Each slice does work in its own way, if you walk that path to the sacred space in your heart, honestly and openly.

Walking to the center of each slice brings you to love, which gifts you with peaceful personal heaven/enlightenment.

True spirituality is love energy. Simple.

John Lennon was damn right when he said "All you need is Love."

♀ Torch Time 2 ♀

Use your flame to bake a pie. Gather only the finest ingredients. Create your own orgasmagical recipe:

Meet the goddess: : Nemetona is the Celtic goddess of Sacred Spaces. Make your own sacred space both inside and outside your heart. This is the oven where you will bake your beautiful pie. Go to that softly vibrating place often.

1. What slice of the religion pie is yours, if any?

_____

_____

_____

_____

2. Are you happy with your piece of the pie? _____

_____

_____

_____

_____

3. If you could change it, what would it look like? Write three traits of your custom religion pie.

_____

_____

_____

_____

4. List three small steps your inner goddess can do now to remake your current piece of the pie into something warm and delicious.

_____

_____

_____

_____

Pain and Panic

Do you dream? I wish it for you if you don't. I dream in glorious technicolor and surround-sound. They are mostly good dreams or everyday dreams these days. Going back, I can remember an occasional reoccurring childhood nightmare, in which I was being chased by a dark man/vampire up a spiral stone staircase. I was an adult before I finally beat that dream. When I was unhappily married, I would dream of sex, nearly every night, with random men. Apparently, since I was in a sexually frustrating marriage, it was my body's way of satisfying its needs. My favorite dreams now are of warm tropical places, in which I am basking in the sun at a beach. Upon awakening I will have such a high vibration feeling of bliss for hours and hours. Then later, as is my routine, I will catch one more glimpse of that dream, seconds before I fall to sleep the following night. Rarely though, do I pick up where I left off. It is a new adventure every night. While researching dreams, I read Dr. Carl Jung's dream books and was inspired to keep a dream journal.

When I was separated from my husband and in a depressed state that summer after my girlfriend died, I would have dreams upon a common theme: frustration. I was burning a big French meal, trying to speak in public but could not make out the words on the script, lost on the streets in some city. One dream even featured me as an older Hindu man escaping from some oppressive military forces via old and squawking trains! Dreams are a way that the universe whispers answers to conundrums to you, in your sleep, and the more powerful or vivid the dream, the more you need to pay attention to it. One of the most telling dreams of that time I remember in vivid detail, because it was so powerful and scary. This dream happened about six months after I left my marriage, and I was still in a very uncertain state. Now, this is quite the glimpse into my mind, and those of you who are schooled in dream interpretation will have a field day with it!

The dream: I left my mother's house, in Maine, and was walking alone down a dirt road in a marshy area that then turned into a tropical setting, in the manner of Jurassic Park. There was a small stream going under the road, which had a guard rail to prevent people from falling in. I stopped and leaned over the guard rail to peer into the water. I saw some fat brown fish the size of raccoons, and I decided to go down and get a closer look at these curious creatures. Standing on a clump of marsh grass, I peered into the rippled waters. Suddenly, out jumped a pair of two-foot long amphibious salamanders. Their slimy skin was mottled gray, and they had very sharp teeth and claws. They kept jumping up out of the water and falling back in while they tried to nip me. Backing up, I leapt to the next patch of grass, and the next. The stream meandered through small interlocking pools, interspersed with mole-hills of clumped marsh grass and hay.

I was now running forward from clump to clump trying to escape the two frenzied creatures, but the water hugged the path. The fiends doggedly followed my horrified flight. These two lizard-like fiends I shall name Pain and Panic, after two characters in the Disney movie *Hercules*. In the distance was an abandoned warehouse. I made for it, manically trying to outrun Pain and Panic, to no avail. I dashed inside the rusted warehouse, and lo, the stream ran right under a rotted wall. I could not outrun Pain and Panic, they were inside as soon as I was.

I scrambled atop a giant boulder in the corner, but Pain and Panic rose ever higher in their leapings. One giant leap, and I felt Pain swirled and suctioned around my forearm and wrist. Then he sank his teeth deeply into my palm. Suddenly I was aware that I had a Swiss Army knife in my other hand, open and ready to use. I slashed at Pain a few times, and caught him in the belly. Panic was still jumping around near my feet, and I leaned over and cut him to ribbons mid-leap. He slid back into the water in pieces. Pain, still gnawing on my palm, was not deterred in the slightest by the gaping hole in his abdomen. So, I frantically cut his thick head off.

The slimy body went limp, and dropped off me. But to my horror, the head lived on! Suddenly it let go of my palm and let out a God-awful animal screeching howl. Then it looked right at me and yelled in a human voice, "You shouldn't have been able to kill me." Slowly the light faded from its eyes to a death darkness, and I whipped that foul head as far from me as I could fling it.

In shock, I sat down on that boulder to decompress. I sat there with my head in my hands for an awful long time in that shadowy building, just breathing. When I had gathered enough energy, I walked out of the building and back into the light.

I was greeted with the yellow police tape of a crime scene. The tape had cordoned off the entire marsh area, and it was filled with people working forensics. Some were milling about with clipboards, and others were lightly scraping the ground with small archeological instruments. The closest one to me turned and stared at me, his mouth gaping. Another, standing near the gaper, spoke to me. "Marie, where have you been?" he asked me, incredulously. I told them I had been resting inside the building for a while. Then they both spoke in unison as they dropped this bomb on me: "You have been missing for eight years."

It was then that I woke up, shocked, from this powerful dream. I will let you, dear reader, interpret this dream. The meaning is pretty evident. Those of you who are old pros in Jungian dream interpretation will get it right away, while those of you who are neophytes will eventually get it if you put down this book for a minute and ponder. (Hint: it is about a girl who conquers her pain and panic, but it is much harder, and takes much longer than expected.)

What I am saying here is to work with your dreams. You think you don't dream? I think maybe you do, but you censor. Figure out how to do it, and listen to the whispers of the universe. This is your intuition. Claim it.

Blue Moon

Listening to the universe is very valuable, and something else very valuable is having another person who actually listens to you. Have you ever had a friend who was like your shrink? I love my friend Elle; she is the best listener I know. And when she speaks, she is a bonafide wordsmith. We met at a job I had many years ago at the local community college. She trained me for my job, and I was impressed with her amazing organizational skills. It was also a great pleasure to see her in action while she went above and beyond to help students. I am not talking about getting the student the correct forms or placed into the correct academic programs. I am talking about helping them down to their very core; changing their lives.

This very rough, blondish woman about forty years old came to Elle's desk, and I was seated close enough to overhear. This woman had just been released from prison, and had very few options, but was bound and determined to get her life on track finally. Before you knew it, this poor soul had told super-listener Elle how destitute she was, how she just really needed a lucky break, and was now ready to change her life. Although I was a bit taken aback by the woman, as she was not the typical student, Elle did not judge, criticize or demean. She listened and took that woman to heart. Over the months, Elle guided her on many occasions, through many confusing processes, and encouraged her every step of the way. That destitute woman's life was radically improved, thanks to Elle.

I think Elle loves the underdog. This is because I think Elle was the underdog as a child, due to circumstances way beyond her control, as was I. Maybe that is the basis of our strong bond. We each know about discrimination. The grown-up Elle now wields a certain power, but she is very tentative and humble about it. I love Elle, and count myself extremely lucky to be one of her close friends all these years.

When I was in the deepest muck of my depression, the first summer I spent divorced, I went to Elle's house for a visit. We sat at her kitchen table, and she told me I looked too skinny. It was true, I had lost about fifteen pounds in a month. I couldn't eat. "Marie, I am cooking you a sandwich and you are going to eat it," she commanded. She forced a grilled cheese sandwich on me. Comfort food. My stomach made extremely loud noises as it finally was getting some sustenance – she heard it on the other side of the kitchen table. "I told you so," she said, wagging her finger at me. Looking back, that grilled cheese saved my life. That woman makes a mean grilled cheese, and an outstanding tuna melt as well.

Tchotchke shopping is one of Elle's passion. Did I mention she is a wordsmith? A Yiddish wordsmith at that. Tchotchkes are trinkets and treasures such as one might find at an antique shop or a yard sale. Whenever we go antiquing for tchotchkes, Elle always chats up the owners. She would be in Utopia if someone bequeathed her a shop of her very own. As for me, a psychic once told me that in one of my past lives I ran an antique shop in England. Yeah, I can see that.

Elle doesn't believe in the goddess tradition. Not many people do, you know. Elle is a little open to it though. Being open to the energy is all it takes. The goddess used Elle as a messenger one day and surprised the heck out of me. That morning, I was sitting at Elle's kitchen table once again. Between us sat a pile of tangled jewelry and mismatched earrings. She had offered to organize and price the jewelry for a favorite tchotchke shop owner of hers. I had stopped in for tea, and offered to help with the crazy pile.

As we worked and the jewels began to be untangled and sorted, I noticed an interesting bracelet break free from the heap. It was silver with light blue stones that had a flash like a moonstone. Elle noticed I kept talking about it, and offered to sell it to me for a deal. Now, I like to live lightly on the earth, and prefer not to be bogged down by too many possessions. I already owned a whole jewelry box of goodies. So I said, "It's pretty, but no thanks."

But for some reason, the bracelet would not leave my mind. Has that ever happened to you? Then there is a reason, believe you me. I searched the stone out on the internet the following day. There was such a thing as a blue moonstone, yes it existed. Not very common. Blue moonstone was the stone of a certain goddess, namely, Aphrodite. My personal goddess. Coincidence you say. Bah! I called Elle up and told her to hold the bracelet for me, I was going to buy it. And on the wicked cheap. Boom. Boom. What shaka-luck!

The bracelet has not left my wrist since. And Elle thinks she is not a goddess. Hee hee. Mazel tov!

Part Two: Going Simply Green

Voluntary Simplicity

As mentioned, when the New Year rolls around each January, I set a goal for the coming year. I have done this forever. I have accomplished ninety percent of these goals. Every once in a while the goal falls by the wayside, but I don't stress about it. I am not that much of a type A personality that I can't just let it go if I don't need it anymore. Past goals run the gamut: learning to speak Italian, buying property in Florida, getting braces on my teeth, going back to college, and so on. So, my goal, that third year of being employed at the church, was to "explore my spirituality," whatever that meant. I didn't even know what it meant; but I planned to figure it out along the way.

When I mentioned my goal to my mother she automatically suggested her religion. I was pretty sure that spirituality did not necessarily mean religion. Oh, I did do the religion rounds on this year-long quest. I went on field trips to several different churches, including the one where I work, a synagogue, and a Buddhist retreat center. Interesting. But what I really did, besides prowling around the church was . . . can you guess?

Yes, I read. I read Deepak Chopra, Sylvia Brown, Edgar Cayce, Caroline Myss, Mike Dooley, Eckhart Tolle, Carl Jung, Joseph Campbell, Thich Nat Hahn and many others. Some were good, some were bad, but there was always at least a piece or two to take away from each, just like in the old saying "take the best and leave the rest." I got books on meditation. I got incense and oils. I looked deep inside myself, and I found my torch was steadily blazing. The flames of my torch now help to light the torches of others, maybe even yours. It will be a life-long journey for me, "exploring spirituality," I am happy to say. So many facets to illuminate and explore.

A previous January for my resolution, I decided after much contemplation, to work on "humility." I didn't really know what it would be all about, but I felt it call to me. How to start? How would you? When I say humility to you, what first springs to mind?

To me it was the humility of Jesus Christ and Mother Teresa. So, in my fashion, I hit the books. I read the New Testament. I read Mother Teresa's writings. I thought of Gandhi, and how he also lived a very humble life after he threw off his business suits and donned his dhoti. While there is no doubt these people embodied humility, it didn't feel as if I was on the right track. I didn't want to become a saint or a martyr, I just wanted to be humble, now, in the current day.

I spoke of my humility exploration/quest to some of my friends. I went to my favorite stone labyrinth in the village, and paced it off, focused on the word "humility." Months had gone by and I still did not have a handle on what I was actually trying to create. Earth Day came, and I was reading some books on carbon-footprint reduction. I came across an intriguing term: Voluntary Simplicity. I liked the phrasing of it. For all my adult life I had often said that I wanted to "live lightly on the earth." That was the exact phrase I had used many a time. "Voluntary Simplicity" captured the essence of my want in a mere two words instead of five.

While talking to my friend Celeste about my new thing of getting into voluntary simplicity, as current-day humility, she said, " I read that book many years ago." That book? My torched flared up. I didn't know there was a book! Boom! What shaka-luck! (Sly and the Family Stone would have been singing about how the "flames are getting higher," if they were with me right then). So I went to the library and took out Elgin's *Voluntary Simplicity*. There it was; what I had been searching for. My goal was now coming into focus. Can you hear the flame on my torch crackling and sizzling? Orgasmagical, oh yeah. I ate that book up. I then read others about radical simplicity, being beautifully slow, and then saw a video about how we all just have too much "stuff."

Had I been duped all this time? The media and popular culture had sucked me right in without any struggle! Dang! Well, the times they were going to be a-changing. Suddenly, it became abundantly clear to me that I need to live less like a blind American consumer, and more like an earth-focused Native-American. I needed to understand that every thing I purchased made an impact. I decided to take steps towards becoming a locavore, a recycler, and a steward of the earth.

I had been unknowingly heading toward this "simple" way for a while anyway. I had been shopping at the local Salvation Army for clothes, books, kitchen ware, and furniture when needed. I had been offering my stuff I didn't want to others for free on Freecycle.com. I had been growing ten different kinds of veggies on my condo porch. I had refused to get cable TV because I was sick of both the relentless advertising, and the horrific "reality" shows that were brainwashing my teens.

It turns out that when you don't spend most of your time forced to work long and hard to get a lot of money to pay for all the stuff you are TV-brainwashed to think you absolutely must have, you then find yourself beginning to get a lot of peace of mind. You get simple. You get humble. You get happy.

When you jump off the consumer treadmill, and embrace Voluntary Simplicity, you have time. Glorious time! Time for relationships, time for appreciation of the wondrous earth, time for practicing humility, time for looking inside yourself— breathing slowly and deeply—and ultimately finding your divine spark. Taken together, aren't all those aforementioned items possibly the big elusive "meaning of life'? Could very well be. Hmm, very big question, and it could very well be the answer.

Voluntary Simplicity: What luck! Boom! Spill some of your torchlight on it, see if you catch on fire like I did when I realized that Voluntary Simplicity is modern-day humility.

Salvation Army
Story of Stuff

If you want to take *your* first steps towards Voluntary Simplicity, something very easy and painless to do is to check out this twenty-minute video on the web: www.thestoryofstuff.org. Annie Leonard narrates this simple line-drawing cartoon that shows you how you got suckered in by the corporate machine. She explains how everything you thought was normal and ok, is actually not. Not by a long shot. You may be wondering right now, how does this "stuff" relate to a spiritual safari? For me, one of the most important keys to finding my inner goddess was to simplify my life in all ways. Less is more. If you bring your goddess torch close by to this one, be careful that you don't set the house of cards on fire. Or perhaps you should purposely burn up all your drama, and see what happens ...

How to simplify your stuff, and the drama that it creates? (Drama robs you of free time to investigate and enjoy your spirituality.) Annie suggests better ways to do some everyday things, and I have taken them to heart. One of them is recycling. And not in the traditional sense of separating paper from plastic and glass. This is large item recycling. Like buying a used car or washing machine instead of a new one, (only if it is energy-efficient). This keeps a still-working car or washer out of the landfill, and stops the corporate machine from exploiting. Exploiting both more raw materials from earth, and also low-wage workers to manufacture a brand new (and unnecessary) one. People have to be sure that the used goods they are buying are not so old as to be energy-hogs, thus negating their efforts, but if done right, a lot of savings can be had. Savings for the planet's resources, and savings of cash in your pocket, too!

A good place to do this alternate type of recycling is at your local thrift shop, or consignment shop, or Salvation Army store, or even a yard sale. You will see the goddesses in there having a blast! What a treat to visit one. Oh yeah. You may see the set of lemonade glasses you used to drink out of at your granny's house in the sixties, or the funky floor lamp your cool uncle had in his groovy pad in the seventies. It is like time traveling. Other more recent things you may find are the items that TV convinces you that you must rush out and buy now. I cannot tell you how many bread machines, George Foreman grills, coffeemakers, DVDs, purses, and other over-bought items line the shelves or sit on tables, just waiting to be adopted into a new and loving home. Think of them like animals at the local shelter, waiting for you to rescue them. Thrift stores save all these still perfectly good items from the dumpsites of our "disposable" society, and this saves you cash while saving the planet. Recycling at its best. Win-win! Now, I am not saying you should cut out buying new goods one hundred percent. How about you take a smaller hit and buy twenty five percent secondhand to start, and see what happens.

Another important outcome of this large item recycling is that by spending less cash, people are then free to earn less cash. The author of *Radical Simplicity*, Jim Merkel, decided to quit his engineering job while on a business trip in Switzerland watching the news of the Exxon Valdez spill. While Jim does not purport to be a goddess, he certainly thinks like one! This newly enlightened man came to the sudden realization that the military weapons he was designing were not helping the world to become a better place. Methodical calculations (he was an engineer by trade) showed him that he could live, and even thrive, on only five-thousand dollars a year income, if he just looked at everything in his life from a different and more sustainable perspective. Pretty radical change for a jet-setting former Yuppie. So that is how he lives his life now.

Well, if he could do it, so could I. Alright, maybe not so radical as he went, but maybe radical enough to be able to live comfortably on a part-timer's salary? He postulates that there is a stigma attached to those of us who only work part-time. I agree. I sometimes feel guilty for only working part-time. Why is that? Many other countries don't live by the forty-hour work week rule. Who said it was a negative way of life? US Corporations, and their nasty habit of only offering health coverage to full-time employees, for one. What would happen to a person who was not pulling his or her full weight on the crazy corporate/consumer treadmill?

What would happen if they only worked part-time at a church office, for example? For starters, they would be penalized by not having affordable company health insurance, and having to buy their own individually, and expensively. Additionally, they would not have as much buying power as the full-timers. They wouldn't be able to afford a TV in every room, or an expensive cable TV package. However, not watching TV, or as much TV, encourages another angle of voluntary simplicity, as it turns out. While taking grad classes in marketing, I watched TV for three nights in a row, as an assignment. I had a stop-watch and timed shows vs. commercials. It was then that I realized that truly the point of TV is to brainwash you out of your cash that you have to work extra hard for, to get extra income to spend on stuff you see on TV. Run that in an endless loop until you are stressed out to the max. When Annie Leonard said it so simply in her little *Story of Stuff* video, it really hit home: You are the donkey chasing the carrot tied to a stick.

Here is another thought. If I don't have a TV in every room, showing me endless commercials, or am not busy out at the mall buying the latest fashions and gadgets, what do I do with my time? I get to spend it living simply on the earth. I get to spend more time at home or with loved ones, because I don't have to generate an overabundance of money. What I do generate is an overabundance of time, and sweet time affords me the pleasure of becoming more spiritual and peaceful. I get to frolic afternoons in a field of dandelions, while other are still strapped to their desks. I redefine my definition of abundance! Removing blind consumerism, trying to impress other people, and entitlement out of the equation, I find that my basic and secondary needs are adequately met and it is much easier to move up Maslow's Hierarchy of Needs chart towards the Self-Actualization tip. So, I choose to work part-time and be simple, green, and guilt free. I encourage a new perspective on successful living: Semi-Radical Voluntary Simplicity for the Average Goddess.

One last thought on embarking on a TV-free diet. As the new millennium rolled around, it seemed there were a million channels, and yet there was nothing on. Things got even worse when my kids became teens. I would find them in a zombie state watching MTV and other reality shows. Wow, what a diet of negative and angry garbage. I began to see the effects in my kids. I took a stand. I cancelled pay TV. I mean all of it. I bought rabbit ears and thus began the great HD TV diet. Three channels were all I could serve up for them. All three were PBS. What luck! TV then became a good thing again. After they got over it, they began to find other things to do with the time they would have been watching TV. Or sometimes they may even watch PBS and learn something new. And what was that, shining in the corner? Did I see a small flicker of flame suddenly appear on their teen-aged fledgling goddess torches? Spark it up, baby!

Porch Gardening

Another delicious, and high vibrational kind of simplicity is that of growing your own food. Even if it is just one lonely tomato or strawberry plant in a bucket, grace happens when you dig in the soil, and care for your crop. Grace happens when you fill your body with fresh and wholesome food. Unbeknownst to us, many of us are filling our bodies with bad food. How can you be a goddess when you are not treating your body like the temple it is?

Have you read Barbara Kingsolver's *Animal, Vegetable, Miracle*? I recently did, and it gave me another kind of enlightened awakening. A food awakening. While I thought I had mostly stayed away from junk food in my adulthood, I was proven wrong. My definition of junk food was rewritten when I read Kingsolver. Over my short lifetime of forty plus years, it seems that real food has been replaced by fake food. Hardly anyone noticed. Food that has been engineered, processed, preserved, and just plain stripped of nutrients. Some things that we eat that are sold as food are actually only one chemical bond away from not being a food, but being a plastic instead. No, I did not make that up—it is a scientific fact. Yuck.

Taking matters into my hands I decided to grow some of my own food. The condo that I had bought in the fall had a nice big south-facing porch. What luck! I gathered up ten large buckets. My good friend, Uncle Tom from my coffee shop clan, delivered ph-balanced soil from his organic topsoil company to my porch. I was ready early. I was psyched! Beautiful, slender seedlings were already sprouting up on my kitchen windowsill. Being a cold-weather veggie, the beets were the first to make the jump to the outside.

The herbs followed, and soon everything was out. There were a few nights when I had to drag it all inside due to frost warnings. We *are* talking New Hampshire here! I lost nothing, and gained a few weeks' advantage. This was great because everything was from seed, I had no flats. The only exception was the tomatoes. I researched heirloom tomatoes to find out what tomato really tasted like a tomato. I had a creeping feeling that I had never really tasted a real tomato. The search was on! I hunted down a Brandywine seedling. Ugly as hell, which is why you don't see it at the big-box markets. It had a stalk on it that reminded me of a puppy with big paws that it will grow into someday Yep, it was gonna be a bigg'un. The thing finally topped out at over seven feet high. I had to nail it to the side of the walls to keep it from kidnapping any of my porch guests.

Also in attendance that year was a small grape tomato, a medium tomato, three green peppers, three large eggplants, a dozen beets, and two stalks of corn for decoration (I had grown from seed in my office starting in February when I just wanted to see something green). I also had two bush beans, two pots of organic seven-seed lettuce mix (cut and come again), and five delightfully fragrant herbs. You might not think that you can grow your own food in such a small space and have it make any kind of impact. But I am here to tell you that you can. All this, and I still had one empty pot!

WANTED: in the village, zucchini seedlings.

This is what I posted on Freecycle.com, and the next day my two new seedling friends were delivered to my office. I applauded when my fellow Freecycler, brought the sprouts through the door (she probably thought I was nuts, but I just have joy). Her husband had grown them from a seed packet, and they had all sprouted. There were too many zucchini seedlings and she didn't have the heart to throw any away. My ad had spoken to her heart. Two Cocozelle zucchini, which I later found out were also heirlooms, joined their new family on the porch. Their spot was clearly in the corner near the bucket containing the two cornstalks with the bush beans at their feet. I heeled in the newly planted seedlings in the empty bucket, and pushed it tight to the corn/bean combo bucket. The three sisters were now complete. I felt like I had to go light some sage to bless the union!

"Locavore" was voted the word of the year that year, and I was on the bandwagon. To be a locavore means to eat local food. A church supper that I was helping to plan at my job brought some sobering thoughts to mind. My fellow green cohort and I were pushing for one of the suppers in the annual series to be an all-local-food supper. We already had a really good supper series going, but the addition of a locavore church supper would raise it to the next level. Now, church suppers have been going on in America since the Pilgrims, when there was no separation between church and State. Imagine a church supper, of say, the year of our Lord 1898: was there any processed orange cheese blocks or gooey marshmallow creme involved? No. So riddle me this: when did church suppers morph from being a locavore meal, involving all local farm food, into a meal topped off with jello-rings that has a carbon-footprint large enough to stomp the whole church, steeple and all, underground by twenty five feet?

My thoughts:

- How did this happen? (Marketing mania of the '50s? "Eat gooey marshmallow creme and you will be cooler than the Jones kid next door.")
- When did this happen? (While I am not blaming the makers of processed orange cheese blocks or gooey marshmallow creme, I am thinking that it happened around the same time processed orange cheese blocks, gooey marshmallow creme, and the classic bologna sandwich were concocted during the baby boom era)
- And why did this happen? (Corporate greed? Fat Cats making fat Americans? Just plain ignorance?)

It actually all happened so slowly over a couple of generations that hardly anyone noticed. So, I have faith that it can be reversed quicker than that, now that people are finally noticing en masse. We are not too far gone; plus, our health, the health of a new generation of diabetic children, and the health of mother earth depend upon it. Nutrition goddesses like Barbara Kingsolver and other enlightened people, like the two fun guys, Ian Cheney and Curtis Ellis, who made the documentary film *King Corn*, have the problem in their crosshairs, and are spreading the word. The new locavore movement can reverse this fiasco. It can save the children and ourselves from problematic health, while saving big on medical bills. Need more proof? Watch the fun documenary No Impact Man, and see how Colin Beavan's wife reverses her health condition.

Don your armor of delicious and fragrant greens, and sally forth! Grow your own porch garden, or join a local farm CSA (Community Supported Association). Eat right, and avoid medications. Eat local and make friends. My porch garden was a wonderful backdrop for many a happy summer luncheon. My goddess friends enjoyed picking the tomatoes off the vine, and plopping them directly on their plate. What delicious luck! Try unclogging your house from stuff, try unclogging your body from junk. Hell, even try unclogging your mind from TV. As we say here, north of Boston, that is "wicked" scary.

♥ Torch Time 3 ♥

Time to simplify. Open the closet door and shine your torch on your clogged up stuff. Bring the torch over to your kitchen pantry. Look at it all in a different light; clogged = complicated, simple = serenity.

Meet the goddess: Coventina is the Celtic goddess of purification and cleansing. Cleansed, purified, and radiant— just like you have the power to be. Close your eyes and see it. See the serenity. Do some of these things, and emerge as a radiant goddess.

1. List three things you can recycle right now:

_____

_____

_____

Stand up and go deal with one of them right now. (Or do it first thing when you get home.)

2. List each room in your house that has a TV:

_____

Which one/s can you donate this weekend _____

Do it. This weekend, go give away one of your TVs (especially the bedroom TV) to the thrift shop, and start to unclog your mind. Put a beautiful live plant on the spot where your TV once stood. Stop every once in a while and ponder the differences between humans and plants. Ponder the similarities. Ponder, ponder, ponder . . .

3. Do you always read the labels before you buy food?

_____

_____

_____

_____

Read books like *Refined To Real Food* by Alison Anneser and Dr. Sarn Thyr, to educate yourself on food choices for you and your loved ones.

Breathing Workshop

A new holistic center was opening close by in the New Hampshire Seacoast area. My adventurous spirit prompted me to go check it out. Scanning through their offerings, a couple of classes caught my eye. One was a breathing workshop. My first thought was: *How funny! Even babies know how to breathe. What is the big deal?* I already knew how to do the Lion's Breath and Lamaze (birthing) breathing. How much more special breathing could there be? Would this class be the biggest waste of money, a giant farce?

Then, I put some more thought into it. Breath is the turning point, the portal between life and death. It is the very first thing you do when you are born, and also the very last thing you do as you die. All through your life, it is breath that lets you enjoy life, and keeps death at bay. Minute by minute. Perhaps it is so ridiculously simple, this breathing, that is it easy to take it for granted. Perhaps, focusing on breathing would be the key to everything?

I called in my reservation, gathered my yoga mat and fuzzy blanket, and off to the center I went. The facility was gorgeous, a beautiful renovated farmhouse in the coastal woods. The owners were very gracious and peaceful. We convened in the Great Room for the session. Ten women sat in a circle on the hardwood floor. After introductions and a brief overview, we lay down on our mats and got instruction on how to breathe correctly. The facilitator discussed various types of breathing, and we tried them all while lying prone. She talked about types of breathing to use while meditating, and about how breathing deeply and slowly can clear out the bad chi. Finally, she discussed three-part breathing. We practiced it, and when everyone got the hang of this odd but powerful breathing, we were ready to begin the real work.

Now comes the good part, brighten your flame so you can see this better: Pulling the blanket over ourselves, and settling in, we started upon a continuous fifteen-minute stint of this three-part breathing. Three-part breathing involves isolating the breath moving through your throat and upper chest, through your lungs, and then way down into the very bottom of your diaphragm. Then back out in reverse order. This breathing is very slow and deliberate. And powerful. In short, it actually does something to you physically: it hyper-oxygenates your blood. I would hazard a guess that it expands your "vibration," and opens a portal for the divine to flow through.

So I lay, struggling awkwardly with this breathing exercise for the first few minutes. Slowly, I finally began to get in the rhythm. Then it became effortless, and the breathing was powerfully flowing through me. I could feel the veins in my legs and arms begin to buzz. I felt consumed by the breathing, and it was gloriously peaceful. My entire body was actually buzzing, my mind solely focused on the buzz. And in some weird way, it was as if I was a light switch, and I had just been switched to the "on" position for the first time. I was so alive, yet so peaceful. Total awareness? Yes, but I was still the usual me this time— no lifting off a couch and floating through the stars.

I could have gone on for quite some time, but the facilitator signaled that it was time to bring ourselves back to a normal breath. Bummer. I was having such a marvelous time inside this breathing pattern that I really did not want to stop. But I did. As we all sat up, she asked for any comments on our experiences. Interestingly, I found that I was the only one in the room that felt a buzz. Odd.

That was the first time I ever felt the natural "buzz." Months later, at a different "Energy Raising" workshop, I felt the buzz again. And sometimes when I am in total focus at Full Moon Meditation, I feel the buzz as well. I like the buzz. How can I describe the buzz? When you've got the buzz, all you wanna do is smile! The buzz makes you happy, light, and free. It's like being drunk, but not on booze. Drunk on a vibration, drunk on a diamond white light. Drunk on joy. Yes, that is it: Joy.

Ah, but all good things must come to an end. Time to go. As I was making my way out the door of the Great Room, I saw one golden box, sitting alone on a shelf of the retail display case. Something made me go over closer to see what it was. What luck! It was Virtue's Goddess

Oracle Cards that I had been searching for. Faster than you can say "who wants to be a goddess?" they were mine. "O, sweet mystery of life, at last I've found you . . ."

That catchy little phrase is actually the first line from this beautiful old tune from 1935, sung in duet. The lyrics continue on, and come right to the point I am trying to make: walking the goddess path brings you to love.

O, sweet mystery of life, at last I've found you
Ah! At last I know the secret of it all;
All the longing, seeking, striving, waiting, yearning,
The idle hopes, the joys and burning tears that fall!
For 'tis love, and love alone, the world is seeking;
And it's love, and love alone, I've waited for;
And my heart has heard the answer to its calling—
For it is love that rules for evermore!

Meeting Celeste

That breathing workshop was very enlightening, so I thought I would keep exploring different workshops and see what else may turn up. Over the internet came a notice about another workshop, this one free, at my favorite metaphysical and circular wisdom bookstore across the state line. As it was December and I was budgeting for the holidays, *free* fell right in my price range, so I reserved a spot.

There were about thirty people in the room when I got there. I quickly tucked into the closest seat and turned my attention to the front of the room. I had misread the email, and so I thought that I was going to a free book lecture/workshop. It turned out the book talk had taken place the week before, and I was now attending an energy raising workshop that was to go on for three hours! Surprise. I have to read my emails more carefully. But as I mentioned, the Universe conspires to assist you. So here I found myself. It was a very diverse crowd.

The main energy worker, Lucia, had assembled a team of people to help with the session. This team was made up of clairvoyants, tarot readers, intuitive, and Reiki healers. There they stood at the front, just looking like ordinary folks. Lucia was a petite woman with close cropped grey hair and a giant toothy smile, like Kenicki in the movie *Grease*. She had the energy of ten women, and she kept it up for the three hours.

She gave a four sentence introduction about energy, and then she was flitting all about the room. She had three or four decks of oracle cards, which she entrusted to one of the helpers who was an experienced reader. The helper pulled ten cards for the group, and laid them down in a line on the carpet in the center of the big circle of chairs were we all were seated in. And then they put one chair in the middle of the circle. For what? The victims, I was sure.

The next hour was a blur of activity as Lucia darted about the room in a running commentary on mingling the energies of all those in the room. She was working like Socrates, asking the crowd about their perceptions, their fears, how they came to have them, if they were *actually* valid still or just old assumptions. Questions. Insights. More questions, rapid fire. People chose cards from the carpet, or maybe the cards chose them. People were up, down, walking around, assigned to the middle seat. It was like a three-ring circus; there was so much going on at all times. Wow! I was fascinated, maybe even overwhelmed. I had no idea what was really going on. But it was not scary at all, and I was very open to soaking it all in.

At one point, I spied one of the psychic helpers staring at me from across the room. She approached. Oh yikes! She stood in front of me and said, "I feel a heaviness." I told her I was a happy person, and had no heaviness, sorrow, or fear, but maybe some confusion as to what was happening here. For that comment, Lucia assigned me to the center seat. The victim chair. Crap.

She gathered the entire crew around me and also asked the folks in the room to concentrate on sending a strong blue beam of energy directly into my ears. How weird is that? So, in silence, this went on for what I felt was an eternity. But the funny thing is, I began to buzz again. I actually got a little dizzy, because I was sitting up this time when I got the buzz. (Lying down is a safer way to be when you get "the buzz," I have found). I was smiling as I made my wobbly way back to my seat.

After an hour and a half, we were allowed a fifteen minute break. Dashing over to the coffee shop, I got a bagel and used the restroom. By the time I got back they were just starting up again. Quickly, I darted straight across the circle to my assigned seat. I was in such a rush that I didn't notice they had laid out a row of new cards on the carpet. I stepped right on one with my big clonking winter boot. Dang! Certainly it was a bad omen, and I would be cursed forever. I apologized profusely to Lucia, and she waved it off. She said there was probably a reason why I had stepped on that card, and to watch that card. Then she winked. I knew right then and there I was destined to meet whoever got that card. I would ask them to coffee and get to know them, no matter who it was. As I said, it was a very diverse crowd.

All right then, in a swirl of energy we started back where we left off. Lucia said "Whoever feels like a card is calling to them, go and pick it up." A handful of people stood up and moved toward the card of their choice. A woman went over and picked up the card I had stepped on. She turned it over and held it out. It was a green card that depicted "Shadow Self." Lucia then told the people holding the cards, "This card is not for you, look around the room and go give this card to another of your choosing."

Curiously, I watched as the card traveled across the room. My card had found its final owner. Who was she? A dynamic woman with expressive brown eyes, short brown hair spiked with blond streaks, and a totally funky leopard print peacoat. Later on in the afternoon the leopard coat lady got assigned to the middle (victim) chair, and I got to get my first glimpse of what she was about. Interesting woman, an artist.

Another quick hour, the workshop was over. The participants were all chatting to each other while they bundled up in their winter coats and scarves. The leopard coat lady was already talking with someone, so I sidled up to the conversation and waited. At a break in the conversation I asked if she wanted to go for coffee the following week. She looked at me kind of strangely, then in a very open way she simply said, "Yes." We traded phone numbers. Over tea in a Starbucks the following week, we realized we were journeying on the same long brown path. We had found each other by the light of our goddess torches. And that is how I met Celeste, now known as the goddess Ixchel, Medicine Woman. What luck!

Masconomet's Grave

Here is a story about strange energies, but not at a workshop. This one was experienced live on an adventurous jaunt that I recently took, but really the story starts about ten years ago. Back then, I was looking for a short-cut, to cut across the backside of one tiny historic New England town and into another. On the map, there was a certain back road that looked like it would be my answer. On that late fall day I was traveling alone down that road, past farms and horses. Soon the houses became further and further apart. Landscaped lawns and tidy stone walls yielded to wild woods. Tangled vines became thick, and the leafless woods had a very old and wild look to them. A shiver ran up the back of my neck. I was experiencing a very odd feeling, like a strong energy force or a foreboding. Whew! I was extremely glad when the homes of the next town started appearing again further up along the roadside. I never forgot that shiver, and that was ten years ago. Freaky, and now here is why.

Many years later I heard from my friend Phil that there was an Native American chief buried in the woods somewhere on the northern outskirts of a certain tiny historic New England town. Jake and I packed a picnic and set off to find it. We figured we would just ask when we got to the town, and surely the townsfolk would point us right to it. Wrong. We asked an old timer at a little store: "I heard something about that. Never been there though. I think maybe it is up at the far edge of town, off of such and such road." We headed to the far edge of town, and we asked people who were walking on such and such road: "No, I never heard of it." We asked a lady riding a horse down such and such road, practically in front of a large iron gate: "No, I have never heard of it, and I ride around here all the time." Hmmm.

We were still stopped in front of that large iron gate, wondering what to do. The gate was right in the area where I had felt such a very sudden, strong feeling all those years ago, and the memory suddenly came back. I told Jake the shiver story. Suddenly, we knew we were in the right place for sure. Turning in, we drove past the gate, up a very steep hill, and to the very end of the road. Nothing. But wait, what was that over there? A small wooden placard stood near the brushy entrance to some kind of clearing in the woods. It looked promising. On that early spring day it was very peaceful, with only the birds singing their new spring songs.

Jake and I stood side by side, solemnly reading the placard about Chief Masconomet and his tribe. It told us how the Agawam tribe was decimated by smallpox, but the chief lived to an old age. With little ceremony, the chief was buried exactly here, when he died in 1658. He was granted this acre on a hill for his burial plot by the King's representative. It remained untouched since then.

The brush and vines intermingled and formed a natural doorway. Past that doorway, there was magic, and Jake and I both knew it. Jake is very open and attuned also. (What luck that we found each other, I am thankful everyday!) Passing through the doorway, tied by slender strings to the perimeter trees, we could see little red cloth pouches filled with something. Charms to keep the bad spirits out, and the blessings in, we surmised. A very large natural stone with an inscription stood at the base of a giant white pine. Lower pine branches swept down from far overhead, almost reaching the ground. Dangling from them like an array of Christmas ornaments were dreamcatchers, beads, feathers, wands, shells, jewelry and other shiny things, and an ode to my old friend Phil (aka, Motorcycle Man, RIP). At the base of the stone was a similar collection of offerings, including a small plastic pony. The whole scene was a mystical and magical delight to the senses. It reeked of respect and love of the earth-ways. We stood silently in the grassy patch for a while, and each thought our own thoughts. Melancholy, magical, and meditative. I was grateful to be there, and especially grateful to be there sharing this with Jake.

As it was still early spring, and the bushes and undergrowth had not won their strangling fight yet, we could see another opening to a path leading into the deep, sacred woods. We went back to the car and gathered the picnic lunch, and then set off down the path. We walked for quite some time. It was a delightfully warm spring day, complete with dappled sunshine, and we journeyed further and further back in time and into the undisturbed woods. It must look just as it did when the Agawams lived on those lands. Finally we came to a vernal babbling brook, a lovely spot for a picnic. I spread out the blanket, and we enjoyed our little picnic, serenaded by the brook. With full bellies and full hearts, we relaxed on the blanket in the sun. You can guess what happened next. The very same thing that has been happening in those woods, and all woods, for centuries. Two naked and natural creatures enjoying each other's fleshly gifts, under the open sky and the warm sun. Only the birds bore witness. The timeless dance ended with a Banchi scream. Boom shaka-laka-lucky . . . Boom shaka-laka-lucky . . .oh yea!

Then, of course, we checked ourselves for ticks.

Dragonfly Glade

The Native Americans and other ancient cultures find meaning in the various creatures they encounter. As a modern goddess, I subscribe to a similar philosophy. According to the medicine men and shamans, animals bring you messages from spirit, and can also lend you their powers. Animal totem poles from the Pacific Northwest are a good example that you may be familiar with. Goddesses, too, commonly have an animal they are associated with. Athena with the owl, for instance. The owl represents wisdom in the Greek culture.

Looking out my back porch one spring morning I saw a large bird land in a nearby pine. Perched on that jutting branch, it observed the skyline for quite some time. When the bird decided to move on, I had my binoculars trained on it. As it lifted on its powerful wings, I saw it was a beautiful red-shouldered hawk. Every now and again I see it in the trees in my back yard, or hear its cry. In some Native traditions the hawk is The Messenger. Hawks symbolize visionary power and guardianship. Hawks tell us to be observant, and to watch keenly for messages. Grateful that I share the same neighborhood with a magnificent hawk, I look for it often. I consider that hawk the personal guardian or the "mascot" of my new abode, keeping my family safe in our condo. By its very presence, the hawk feels like a good blessing.

More animal blessings came my way later that summer. From reading, I learned that to be able to meditate or pray more deeply, a person should try to find themselves a personal "sacred space." This space could take any form; indoors, outdoors, sparse or congested. The only qualifier is that is has to be some place close by that you can access easily. Once settled on a space, it should be visited often, almost daily if possible. The more time spent there, the more powerful the space becomes. When I moved to my condo, I began the search for such a place. Eventually, I came to realize that this space, my personal chapel so to speak, would be in the woods once inhabited by Native Americans, beside the large drumlin lake.

Now, this place is a large conservation area, so there was plenty of land to choose from. Too much! I stopped here and there, and tried out different spots. One, under the shade of a pine grove, was too deep in the forest, and too buggy. Another, high up on a solitary rock, had a beautiful water view. Alas, it was too hard on the butt, and too out in the open. I needed to feel more sheltered, more hidden, while still having a gorgeous view of the water. Other people should be able to pass by without noticing me. I needed to find a nook by the water's edge to tuck myself into.

One sunny summer day, while walking alone near the access road, I came upon the perfect spot. Just off the right side of a secondary trail, and behind some grass and scrubby bushes, there were some flat rocks near the water's edge. Passing through the grass and standing on the flat rocks, I could then see more rocks to the left, leading downward somewhere behind a wall of sumac. Clambering over an easy ten-foot stretch of rock and a fallen tree trunk, I was then at the last rocks on the bank. The rocks were smooth and rounded, and gently sloped toward the water's edge, making it comfortable to sit, and even lean back.

Kicking off my sandals, I leaned back and relaxed, my face full in the sun. Walkers on the trail, behind and above me, would occasionally pass by chatting. I could hear them candidly speaking to each other, and they never had an inkling I was sprawled out in my sunny nook just below them! The spot was perfectly hidden.

The first special thing I noticed about what I now call my "happy place" was an interesting rock, just next to the combination of rocks I was using as my lounge chair. It glinted a deep, rusty gold in the sun. Millions of tiny layers of mica were compressed with unusual rusty golden sand, and when I pressed a tiny chunk of it between my fingers, it disintegrated into golden fairy dust. Making wishes, expressing gratitudes, and asking for blessings, I flicked shot after shot of the golden powder into the sun, where it exploded in firecracker fashion and disappeared. Small, dark fish, lazily basking in the sun-drenched waters less than a foot deep at the edges , enjoyed the show.

When I finished playing with the sparkly fireworks, I lay back still and looked up at the blue sky. Complete peace washed over me as I lazed in my hidden lagoon, breathing in the simplicity of the moment. To the right of me lay a fallen tree trunk. It blocked the entrance to this secret path, with its rotted tips half in and half out of the water. To the left stood a big bushy and twiggy shrub, which for some reason grew directly in the shallows. Directly in front of me was a clear view of the lake, the shoreline swaddled in lily pads with tiny pink flowers.

It was then that they came.

Red ones, blue one, green ones. Huge ones and tiny ones. Flitting to and fro on their glinting gossamer wings. Stopping in midflight to alight effortlessly on a fractured branch of the fallen tree. Chasing each other around and around the twiggy bush. They paid me no mind, as they went about their ethereal lives. My happy place is a natural dragonfly glade. What luck!

In shamanic speak, dragonflies represent female wisdom, and transition. A dragonfly lives the first two years of its life as an underwater creature. In the third year of its life it undergoes a radical change, and takes to the air! These beautiful creatures remind us that we ourselves are not limited to what we have always known ourselves to be: we too can manifest a radical change. "Look past the illusion of the moment, then work to simplify and become your authentic self," is the message of the dragonfly. This dragonfly glade is the place I chose as my sacred space, or, perhaps, it chose me. What luck! There are twenty miles of trails in this conservation area with its huge drumlin lake. What did make me look off the path at that particular spot and notice those flat rocks behind the sumac trees anyway?

♀ Torch Time 4 ♀

Explore new facets of your simple self with laser focused intention. Let your inner goddess sparkle:

Meet the goddess: Diana is the Roman goddess of Focused Intention. So are you now. Focus on your inner search for spirituality, and you will hit your mark. Focus on these two verbs during your search: Explore and Observe.

1. List three odd, curious, or adventurous spiritual classes/events/projects you have thought about doing:

_____

_____

_____

_____

Why have you not explored any of them yet? _____

_____

_____

_____

_____

What you just wrote above was an excuse. Figure out a way to make at least one of them happen, regardless, then go explore.

2. List three possibilities for your own sacred "happy space" where you can go and think, or just be:

_____

_____

_____

_____

Spend time this weekend trying them out until one fits. Look around, observe what visits you there.

3. Is there an animal that appears to you often? Did you just see an animal in the oddest place?

_____

_____

_____

_____

If so, perhaps it has a message for you. Check the internet for the meaning of various animal totems.

Green-Eyed Lady

She liked to say that she changed my first diaper. Ann-Margaret was ten years my elder, and our mothers were neighbors. Because she was older, she could tell me stories about myself that I couldn't remember, or explain to me the back story about something before my time that would help me to understand certain family dynamics better. All I could remember from my very earliest times with her were snippets, like hearing "The Age of Aquarius" blasting through the speakers at her high school graduation in the Massachusetts fishing village where we grew up, or seeing her shiny black hair blowing in the salty wind as she marched my sisters and me across town, in our Easter dresses, to attend the egg hunt at the local park.

While ten years is a giant chasm of a gap in age when you are in school, it is not that much of an issue when you get into your twenties and beyond. Needless to say, we were like sisters. We were in each other's inner ring of VIPs (very important people). Because she was older than me, I looked to her to mentor me through many of life's challenges. She had moved for her career to Washington, DC, but I would call her for advice, or to tell her the latest news, or just to hear her voice.

Even with the move, we saw each other a lot, because she was a school teacher with summers off at the same time I was a stay-at-home mom with two small girls. And we both loved the beach; many of our best conversations took place on a beach. She loved that Bette Midler movie, *Beaches*, and made me see it. I hated it. So sad! Every spring we made our plans for the summer, which would always include traveling up and down the US East Coast, from Kitty Hawk to Bar Harbor and everywhere in between. One spring she thought she had developed a pesky case of bronchitis. But no, after the doctor checked he said it was advanced cancer, and he gave her six months to live.

Shock does not begin to describe it.

Through her sheer will-power and stubbornness she beat that six month verdict. She beat it by a mile. She was always a powerful Leo woman. She beat it so well, that it took me by surprise when she suddenly took a turn for the worse after two years and went into the hospice facility. Two days before she was admitted, I slept in her bed with her, like we had done many times before on various vacations and family gatherings. We talked a little while lying there and she told me that it was important that I "get religion." I had no reply, as usual, for she was a very vocal born-again Christian and would periodically get on me about it. I was practiced at ignoring what I perceived as her recruitment overtures. Well, that night it was a very light sleep for me, and a medicated sleep for her. We had to get up once or twice in the middle of the night to change bandages and sheets. Her mother, a retired nurse, was sleeping in the next room and kept the schedule flowing.

She got more medicated at the hospice every day. On my third visit, I had been in the room for fifteen minutes when the aide asked for my assistance to adjust the pillows. I moved closer to the bed and took hold of Ann-Margaret's left arm and guided her forward so the pillows could be propped up. My dying friend suddenly came out of her morphine stupor; her green eyes caught mine and recognition flowed into her. I saw her pupils widen. She surprised me as she chirped a cheery and energetic "hi." Like the kind of "hi" that you would say if you were shopping at the market and came around the corner and suddenly was face to face with a friend.

It was as if in that millisecond she was so surprised to see me that she forgot about where she was; all tubed-up, doped-up, and trussed-up in that hospital bed. Things were normal again for her for one millisecond, she was greeting a friend, and I think that was a relief to her. One burst of energy. And that was all. One old, regular, happy, "hi."

But in the next millisecond, all her pain and sadness flowed back in to her, and she sank back into the bed and back deep inside herself. No more words, just straining breath.

Footsteps in the hall signaled a group of musicians from her church that had come to sing and play her some favorite hymns. As the musicians filed in with their guitars, I quickly excused myself to all in the room and headed to my car. I looked at the last musician as I passed by; his eyes were flowing with silent tears, as were mine.

That is the last time I saw my friend of forty years. She died less than twenty-four hours after the hymns. This event took place one month after my marriage of eighteen years dissolved and I moved out. Times were very dark for me then. The loss was huge.

I missed her and wanted to feel her spirit. But I never did. I looked in all the places we would go, but she was not there. I looked for her in my dreams; she was not there. One of her favorite things to do was to watch the fireworks. We had seen them together in Bar Harbor, Gloucester, Rockport, Boston, DC, Williamsburg, Rehoboth Beach, and Kitty Hawk and countless other places over the years. On July Fourth, I went alone up to the bell tower at the church, high above the deserted and darkened village downtown.

There I sat, all alone, at the highest point in the village. I could see a half-dozen displays of far away fireworks popping up everywhere in surrounding towns and well beyond towards the coast. The mosquitoes had not yet traced me so high up in my perch. I had not turned on any lights in the church or tower, as to not draw attention. It was hot and muggy and the silent downtown lay far below me, dead still. Vapor hung in the thick air.

I desperately wanted to feel her, or hear her. I was at a total loss in my life, and I wanted her to tell me what to do. I was so very sad. Intensely sad. If ever I was going to get a message from a loved one passed, it would have been then. But, nothing. Dead nothing. Climbing down all the ladders and staircases, after almost an hour of waiting, I realized that beyond a doubt, I was on my own. That was in my pre-torchlit days. I was in the dark.

Such a funk had descended upon me that I now believe I was clinically depressed for the two months following her death. It was a horrifying experience. Thankfully, it was not chronic.

By some strange coincidence (read synchronicity here and scream out "Boom. What shaka-luck"), on July fifth I saw a flyer in a village shop window advertising Salsa dance lessons. Figuring why not? I signed up for a six-week session on Thursday nights. I had read that in ancient Greek times, dancing (together with drinking wine) was prescribed for those having a rough time. I am not kidding! Since I am not into hard drinking, I decided to give dancing a try. My depressing funk would stay with me all week, but would lift about ten minutes into the lesson, and leave me until the next morning. Sweet respite.

Jewell & the Ballroom

After completing my six-week lesson, the instructor invited the class to go to the local ballroom, in a New Hampshire Port city to the north, for a social dance. I decided to go. Dancing shoes strapped to my feet, I boldly punched the gas pedal and headed north on the highway that Friday night. Oh, I was brave. I had no idea what I was getting myself into, but I didn't care: dance lessons were over, and I needed more to keep the funk at bay. Actually, after I had parked and looked at the front of the building, I got less brave suddenly. Perhaps going for a quick beer at the micro-brewery up the street might boost me back up? I went and it did. I guess those Ancient Greeks were right!

And that is how my ballroom experience began. I had such fun that night. Everyone was very friendly and helpful (and no one laughed). They showed me steps to the dances I didn't know, like foxtrot and swing. I went back the next Friday night, and the next. Ballroom dancers are fantastically friendly and fun people. You can visit any ballroom across the county, and have a wonderful and warm experience. If you know the steps, you are in, and it is not scary at all.

I often liken it to pick-up basketball. If you know the rules, you can just jump right in anywhere in the US and make friends. Probably in other countries as well; dance overcomes the language barrier! I have been to ballrooms in three states now, and it is always guaranteed to be a fun night. So, if you have been thinking about learning to dance, I say go for it. What is holding you back? As you can see from my little tale here, there is nothing to worry about. Only good things happen at ballrooms. They are magical places. What luck! And goddesses dwell there, as well as a few Lords of the Dance. And the Samba beat goes Boom ba ba Boom . . .

Once you get a good feel for the beat of different dances at the ballroom, you begin to hear that beat in music you have known for years. For example, a lot of the faster Elvis Presley tunes are swing. A great many Frank Sinatra tunes are foxtrots, and Carlos Santana has many familiar cha-chas. Oye como va! These rhythms can be found in today's hit tunes as well. My favorite band of the moment is De Sol, a Latin rock band from New Jersey. Their CDs are full of my favorite dance beats; salsa, cha-cha, meringue, rumba. I blast them in my car all the time. Plus, judging by the lyrics on *Lady Karma* and some of their other tunes, I think that Albie and the rest of the band are in touch with their inner goddesses!

Speaking of goddesses: the first time I laid eyes on Jewell she was on the dance floor wearing a slinky red velvet gown with flames running across the bodice, leg slits up to there, and a super hot-pair of red strappy shoes. She is a tall, slender, and striking woman, with what you might call "presence." Those long pale legs afford her a very graceful style when she dances ballroom. She is a delight to watch.

And she is a delight to know. Turned out that she lived in the village center too! We became great friends in no time. She has such panache` and joie de vivre. You might mistake her for a Nordic goddess if you saw her on the street in one of her fabulous stoles or capes, striding tall with her spiky grey hair and pale hazel eyes glittering against her milky white skin. A very sexy woman indeed. Never mind that she has five grown children.

As you may have guessed, she is my good friend, the goddess Freya: Nordic goddess of fertility and celebration.

The Milonga

You are invited to a very significant, not to be repeated, Birthday Milonga for Jewell, read the invitation. How excellent! A milonga is a certain kind of dance event. It is similar to being invited to a Sock Hop. You pretty much know the night is going to be all about Jitterbug and Twist. The milonga is about Tango. Red hot tango; tango shoes, tango dresses, tango hairdo with a big flower. My Argentine Tango was not all that good, but I figured if I wore a swingy enough dress, no one would really notice. (I wore my black dress that is like the white one that Marilyn Monroe wore when she stepped on a vent.) Plus I knew the DJ would play a little Salsa to mix things up, and that I could really dance. I was ready to go.

Except for a date. At the last minute Jake bowed out, and I put in a call to my friend Faith (the goddess Kali), and said " How would you like to go to a hot party tonight?"

She sounded tired. She said she was planning on staying in that night to rest. She asked what the party was all about and I told her: tango. She was not a ballroom dancer, but had taken some Salsa lessons. She hesitated. I insisted. "Why don't you just stop by for a half hour or so, wish Jewell a Happy Birthday, then have a glass of wine and leave? I hear she is having quite the spread of food, too, if you are hungry. Maybe some guy will gallantly volunteer to teach you a tango step or two. It could be fun."

There was silence on the other end of the phone. Finally, she said to me, " Marie, I drew a message card tonight and it said *Spontaneity*, so I guess I have to go. What does one wear to a milonga?"

"Dress like you are going to the ball."

"You mean wear a long gown? I don't have one."

"No, you can't really dance in a full-length gown. Wear a knee-length swingy dress that is pretty formal." I then gave her directions, and told her I would be working the front door buzzer for the first half hour. I would go up to the party when she got there.

I got there early, as I had promised Jewell to work the buzzer on the door. The event was to be held after hours in the swanky offices of the old-money investment firm in the Port city, where Jewell worked. For security reasons the building had quite the elaborate system to allow entrance. I worked it for the half hour, buzzing many guests through, before Faith arrived.

The door buzzed in a stunning blonde woman dressed in slinky red. I didn't even recognize her at first. "Faith, you are one sexy bitch!" I yelled, when "light dawned on Marblehead." (This is a phrase we use up here, north of Boston a pun on name of the village of Marblehead, and your own thick skull.)

"Why, thank you," she sassed back. We sashayed over to the elevator, arm in arm, and got in. By the end of the soiree she had danced the night away, and had two offers for dates. Ah, sweet mystery of life . . . And this is all because she listened to her *Spontaneity* card. What luck!

Back to the party though, because this was Jewell's big, significant, not to be repeated birthday after all. Let us not forget that fact. And Jewell embodies Freya, Nordic goddess of fertility and celebration. Let us not forget that fact either. She was red hot that evening! What a fantabulous soiree that night was. It just went on and on and on. The food was superb, the wine delectable, the music outrageous. Couples swirled all around the dance floor in their finest form. I got some great shots of Jewell dancing tango in her red dress with the black fringe.

Towards the end of the evening, I sat down to relax in a wing chair just off the dance floor. Aphrodite was pooped! The shapes, shadows, and sounds of tango fanned out before me. Across the way, I could see Jewell and her partner of the moment (everyone wanted to dance with the birthday girl) in tango embrace, moving through the other dancers. She was smiling in a dream-like fashion. I think she was glowing a little in that darkened room. Suddenly, such a wave of joy washed over me that it brought tears to my eyes. I cried tears of joy for one of my best friends, who was having the night of her life! It was completely satisfying. I got up right then, and went over and just hugged her. Oh, what a night!

Sitting in front of my computer the next day, I uploaded the pictures of the party. There was Jewell, Faith, and myself all posing arm-in-arm in our fancy dresses. There was Faith, all smiles next to one of her new dates. There was Jewell, dancing tango. But wait, what was that in the picture?

Most marvelously, quite miraculously, there was a ring of tiny sparkles floating around her as she danced. I have been told that when odd little sparkly orbs like that appear in a photograph, it is an angel. A host of angels were dancing with delight around Jewell that night. Amen, sister goddess.

♀ Torch Time 5 ♀

Shine your torch on the disco ball, and watch the spangles float in the air! Dance like nobody's watching!

Meet the goddess: : Yemenya is the African Sea-Goddess of Golden Opportunity. She urges you to walk through the open doors. Just do it! Can't find someone to do it with you? No matter. Do it yourself or join a local group of enthusiasts via www.MeetUp.com.

1. List three fun things you used to do, and miss doing:

_____

_____

_____

_____

2. List three fun things you always wanted to do:

_____

_____

_____

_____

3. List three people, or types of people, you wish were your friends:

_____

_____

_____

_____

Take action on making one answer from each question a current reality.

Extra Credit: Can you match up a new friend to a fun activity? Ask them and find out!

Part Three:
Plant Spirits

The Tea Shop

A new shop opened in the village, directly across the street from my office. It was a tea shop. How lovely, I thought; I will have to go there for tea and crumpets with my friends and family. My mother and sisters and nieces visited shortly thereafter. On that cold frozen day, we headed to Willow's Tea Shoppe for a special treat. The décor was clean and modern, tiny sparkling lights and beautiful music filled the air. Spiced chai was on special, and there were many traditional favorites such as Earl Grey, on the handwritten chalkboard.

As I stood there looking, I noticed that behind the counter were rows and rows of glass jars filled with assorted dried leaves and powders. Hand-written labels were marked with names like Graceful Lady, Chill Out, and Peaceful Journey. Other jars were labeled with names of ingredients like arrowroot, skullcap, cat's claw, or chicory. Interesting. I ordered Peaceful Journey, to see where that would take me.

After discussion with the woman behind the counter I was informed that Graceful Lady would help with symptoms of PMS, and Chill Out would help to decongest during a flu. Peaceful Journey was alleged to mellow you out and relax you. I was up for that, especially with a big gaggle of my family in town. I had heard about teas with medicinal properties, but had never seen them being sold boiling hot at a shop before.

That tea was wonderful, and it did give me quite a relaxed feeling. One cup of tea led to a relationship with the owner, Willow, which was to last for years. During particularly bad colds I would stop by the shop for a steaming cup of Sinus Relief or Chill Out tea. I couldn't get enough of that soothing brew. I was hooked.

A couple of years later, in the shop to get my relaxation fix (with my new favorite, Fairy Flowers, a mix of six flower petals) I asked if

Willow could recommend a homeopathic doctor. I thought I would like to check in about my chronic sinusitis before winter rolled in. As she checked through her files for a phone number, she ticked off "Naturopath doctors," "Holistic doctors," "Acupuncturists" and more. Just as she ran down the list, I realized that in my ignorance, I had asked for the wrong thing.

What I was looking for was some kind of natural doctor that would get to the root of my sinus headaches. Over the years, my regular primary care physicians would see me for five minutes, prescribe me an antibiotic, then shoo me out the door. I wanted more. I wanted to be healed: mind, body, and soul. Goddess style.

As Willow was sliding her finger down over the numbers on her list, I stopped her. "Excuse my ignorance, but think I am confused. All I really want is someone who can help me heal my sinus naturally, once and for all. I think I am using too narrow a word when I say Homeopathy."

She looked up from her list. "I can help you. I have helped many others with sinus complaints. I look at you as a whole person to see how everything is interacting, and then suggest herbs that could help you."

What luck! She was exactly the one I was looking for.

"How silly I am, Willow, I have been coming here all this time for tea, and never realized what you really did. Here, I thought you just sold tea, and now, I realize that you are an herbologist!"

"Herbalist," she corrected me, "I specialize in teas and herbal medicine, and I also work with plant spirits."

Plant spirits? Was there such a thing? Get your torch ready. Interesting concept. I took a form to fill out at home, and made an appointment to see her for a consultation. I also joined her email newsletter list.

The Weed Walk

The email newsletter from Willow's Tea Shoppe said. "Sign up now for a guided weed-walk with the herbalist. See common plants in the village center, and learn their various uses." That piqued my interest, so

I signed up. The day came and it was blazing hot. I donned my lightest sundress, my straw hat with the wide brim and hoped for the best. Armed with my camera, a notebook, and a bottle of water, I headed out the door of my condo into the noon heat of an August day. The very high heat that day had reduced the number of participants to two: myself and a hardy teen-aged girl. In the air-conditioned shop, Willow introduced us to each other, and told us the walk would take about two hours. Fearlessly, we stepped back out into the relentless heat, water bottles in hand. First stop: the parking lot.

I was amazed to find out that most of the common weeds along the roadside are not weeds at all, but herbs. Medicinal herbs. An herb can be loosely defined as any non-woody green plant that dies down to the ground after flowering. For centuries, many of these herbs were carefully grown and tended in people's home gardens. Many "weeds" you see in abandoned lots or along the road are refugees from long-gone gardens. The village has a plethora of old stately homes whose gardens no longer include these herbs. The herbs are wily though and they have survived through the centuries on their own, and with the help of little animals and the wind.

By the 1940s the growing pharmaceutical industry was full of promises to eradicate mankind's ills. This was done in the lab by isolating the active ingredient of a plant, and reproducing it chemically. The problem with that can be deduced by reading the long list of side effects that come with each drug. The whole plant has buffers so side-effects are rare.

Prior to World War II, medicine was mostly teas, ointments, and poultices made from plants. Druggists had big glass jars filled with dried herbs on shelves behind the counter. Colonial and Victorian housewives grew the most common medicinal plants in a separate section of the garden. Many of these plants were brought over from Europe, and then acclimated here in America (and now grow wild.) Even before that, the Native Americans had been using indigenous plants for centuries. One cannot tell anymore which plants are native or not, as they all share the same space in the abandoned parking lots, by the edge of the river and the road, and as garden weeds.

Willow showed us common weeds that can be eaten: dandelion, violets, chickweed, lady's thumb, burdock, and red clover, which is actually pink. (I am sure you have seen the pretty pinkish-purple flowers shaped like poms-poms many times over.) Red clover flowers affect "hot flashes," as they contain phyto-estrogens. Burdock, she said, is also very commonly used as medicine. Full-grown, it stands about waist-high and has small purple flowers. It also has those fat round burrs that get stuck on your cat or dog's underbelly, and get so caught up that you have to use scissors to hack off a hunk of fur. The burrs also stick to each other in a suspiciously Velcro-like manner. As a matter of fact, it was the inspiration for that product. The first year-root of the burdock is "gobo," the Japanese wonder vegetable reputed to lower cholesterol, among many other uses. Violet flowers and leaves can be tossed into salads, and create a nice look. More importantly, the leaves can be ground into a poultice and pressed against a cyst, to shrink it. Beautiful weeds were everywhere our eyes fell: St. John's/Joan's Wort (to combat depression), yarrow (for regulating blood flow), Queen Anne's Lace (the seeds are used for natural birth control!).

On and on the tour went, full of information just like that. Willow very briefly introduced us to about twenty-five plants that all goddesses should know about to stay healthy. She cautioned that one should be very clear on the plants they are harvesting, and in fact, use a guidebook when in any doubt at all. So much to know, and that was just plants on the side of the road *in a small space of a quarter of a mile!* It was truly fascinating. My eyes were certainly opened that hot and humid afternoon. Since then I see edible and medicinal plants everywhere: around the lake by my condo, in parking lots everywhere, by the edge of the roads, and many, many other places. I love those weeds!

Hmm, now that I think about it, the first books I ever took out of a library, back when I first learned to read, where children's stories about good witches making love potions and happy brews. I have always gotten a kick out of stories and movies that involve magical potions made from eye of newt and Puck with his magical love flower in Shakespeare's *Midsummers Night's Dream.*

They say your old soul is attracted to what it knew. A psychic once told me that in one of my past lives I was a Seminole Indian woman.

Maybe I once heard the plants speak. Did you know that plant DNA is tremendously more complex than human DNA? Plant spirits? Fascinating. You never know . . . bring that torch over here so we can further investigate.

Pipe Dreams

Mugwort (aka, cronewort) was one of the herbs that I was introduced to that day by Willow. It has a certain smell that vividly reminds me of my youth. Run your hand up its long slim stalk, and the fragrance will cling to you in the same way a tomato stalk smell does. It is earthy and musky. Mugwort thrives in the poorest conditions. This is the plant you will see rising up through cracks in the pavement of abandoned parking lots. It can be seen standing shoulder high, in massive droves along the back roads. Mug is a glass, and a wort is a plant. This plant was once used to brew beer. It can also be brewed into tea or dried and smoked, or put in a sachet under your pillow; it is alleged to induce vivid dreams, lucid dreaming, or just better dream recall.

I dream multiple times every night, and I can usually remember them upon waking. This is good. Really good. But maybe I could do better? Could I achieve lucid dreaming? Could I get more in touch with my inner goddess with the aid of herbs? Research shows that the still point between being awake and falling to sleep is a portal for the elusive out-of-body experience I wanted to achieve again. Out by my mailbox I picked a mugwort stalk, and put it under my pillow for a few nights to see what would happen. I did dream those nights, but not anymore than usual. Disappointing! I brewed it up with an African Rooibus tea, and drank it one afternoon. Relaxing to be sure, but no lucid dreams. One last method to try: smoking it. But how? I had no paraphernalia. Then it hit me, I must get a pipe. Not just any pipe, but something completely natural, like a peace pipe.

While researching mugwort and peace pipes on the internet, I came upon a very interesting Web site that sold organic smoking herbs. Well, what about that! I ordered the twenty-two pack mega-herb sampler. Twenty-two legal smoking herbs, smoked by Native Americans and artists like Poe (to induce creativity), were on their way to my door.

What luck! I mentioned this to the goddesses, and they were all very interested. We could have our own sacred ceremony. But for one thing: no pipe. I was on a mission now.

No luck at the Native American & Meditational Goods store a few towns to the north. But the owners were going to Arizona next month, staying for a month, and they would bring back more stock. Hmm, a two-month wait? Next.

On a different day I tried a pipe and tobacco store, to the south and three towns over, on crowded US Route One. Upon entering the establishment, I choked. Four older gentlemen, seated in wing chairs, were languidly puffing the afternoon away like Alice's blue caterpillar with its hookah. This was man-land. I deduced they must have been hiding out from their wives.

The shop was like a Willy Wonka candy store for cigar and pipe smokers. It was all clean and shiny and bright, and had tons of pipes, tobaccos and other goodies for the well-appointed smoker squirreled away in every possible nook. The four gentlemen in the circle of wing chairs were clearly enjoying this slice of smoker's heaven on earth, and they paid my gasping no heed.

I was getting dizzy trying to hold my breath whilst looking around for a pipe, when *he* came out of the back office. Lordy, lordy, it was Willy Wonka himself! I actually giggled when I saw him, he was such a delight to behold! This long, tall drink of a man, with an elegantly curved briar pipe clenched between his teeth, was from another, more genteel, era. He sported tan slacks, and a matching tan striped vest adorned with a golden-chained pocket watch draped across his breast. The starched white sleeves of his cuff-linked dress shirt matched his perfect white handlebar moustache, which was generously waxed to two perfect, jaunty points. With twinkling eyes, he told me he had no peace-pipe styles in the store, and did not know where one could be obtained. This humble man was a delightful time warp. I wanted to stay and look at what he did have, and chat with him, but my oxygen was running out fast. Thanking him, I fled back to my car, and tried to shake off the embedded smoke. Next!

The continuing quest for a natural pipe led me to what was called in the 1970s, a Head Shop. What a blast from the past—wow! Glass-blown pipes, in the shapes of scorpions, octopi, and various other creatures, bongs, hookahs, and your basic steel or stone pipes. But nothing like what I had in mind. I was at my wit's end, and did not want to order online a fancy ceremonial peace-pipe, made out of deer antler with eagle claw. Acquiescing, and wishing for this quest to end, I settled for a natural corn-cob pipe, unvarnished cob and pure wood stem. It cost me all of five bucks. My plan was to pimp out that pipe with rawhide fringe, beads, shells, and feathers. By the time my shipment of the twenty-two pack mega- herbs arrived, she would be ready. The goddesses would be having some crazy good dreams. Yippikio!

Breathe

Dreaming is very relaxing. But dreaming is relegated (mostly) to the nighttime. What about the daytime? That is where the stress occurs. A way to relax in the daytime, is to just get simple.

How to get simple? Slow down and soak it in.

How to slow down? Just stop, and start to breathe, and you just may awaken to what is inside you.

The simplest act, breathing, is your key to unlock some pretty amazing miracles. Dedicate yourself to becoming a connoisseur of breathing, and you will soon begin to understand! Breathe when you are happy, and breathe when you are sad. Breathe when you are lonely, and breathe when you are crazy busy.

Intentionally breathe slowly seven times. Repeat that seven times in one day, for seven days. I call it the 7/7/7 method. Do this without thinking a single thought. A blank mind. Easier said than done, you will find! If your mind really really needs something to hang on to, then slowly count the breaths. (Keeping count is the maximum thought you are allowed to have during this exercise.) After the seven days, a micro spark may flicker on your torch. The non-believers are saying to themselves at this point, "Surely you jest!" But no, it is true. This breathing meditation simply slows you down.

Once you cut out most of the outer distractions, you will soon begin to notice inner things. You will eventually "hear" your insight.

Hearing your insight, leads to a strengthening of your intuition. And intuition is your divinity in action. It sure sounds divine!

After I became aware of this progression, I became calm, sure, and magical. My eyes were opened to the ways the universe gifted me, the fledgling goddess, to the lucky things it offered. My torch was lit. Practice breathing, and your goddess torch will be lit and reveal to you the lucky things, even in the things that you may at first consider weird or unlucky.

Sometimes, when life is really stressful, even breathing can be difficult. Goddess or not, there will still be times in your life when you can't breathe, maybe even for weeks, but it will pass.

The good news is that being a goddess will give you a calm, sure, and magical confidence that will get you through the absurd, rotten, stinkin' parts of life with grace. Those stinky parts are big luck for you, in hindsight. Sometimes something horrible, like a big bowl of ugly, is what is needed to get you unstuck. If your journey is steeped in uncertainty, and you feel like you are going to break your ankle in the dark at any moment, lean on your sister goddesses. If you can't find any local goddesses quite yet, you can sign up for monthly eZines from wise-women goddesses like www. SusunWeed.com and others.

In the end, you will find it was rather simple to go simple. Go figure.

According to herbalist Rosemary Gladstar, herbalists who used a single herb at a time were once called "simplers." I love the term! She says simplers " understood the basic laws of life and learned through common sense and experience." Goddesses are modern-day simplers too, of a sort. If you are reading this book, perhaps you are already on your way to becoming a simpler of this century. If so, it would help if you too could find some of us other goddess-simplers to hang with. Where to look? You can find us at the churches, the meditation places, the woods, the healing-arts schools, the tea shops, and the metaphysical bookstores. Or you can also just go online to get started. Come join us. When you do, you may find, like I did, that suddenly you've got goddesses galore on your sacred journey. On your simple journey. On your miraculous journey. And the companionship makes the journey a lot more fun! Yea, baby.

Green Witch

I had seen her Wise Woman Web site, and couldn't wait to soak in all the information there on herbs. Ooops! There were over 3000 pages: this would take some time. Running through her calendar, I noticed she was coming to the New England coast to speak and lead a weed-walk. What luck! I had recently gone on the weed-walk with Willow, and Willow had learned her herbs, in part, from the Wise Woman Weed. I really wanted to meet her, to feel her vibe and see if it was for real.

Susun Weed went to UCLA in the groovy '60s, where a chance encounter (read luck) led her to study medicinal herbs and Native American practices all over the country. She currently resides in Woodstock, NY, with her goats and weeds, where she teaches. Very groovy. Plus she can hear the plants speak. She understands their spirits. Oh, that my ears would someday open!

Bedecked in a red bandana with matching red jeans and a black tee shirt depicting a wolf, she stood barefoot on the beach on one of the very last days before the autumnal equinox. The bandana held down her graying black hair, which was wild with her animated movements. She opened with a song in a voice that sounded like a cross between a Native American chanter, and a gospel hymnstress. An old and wise voice, like the voice of a tree on planet Pandora.

Susun Weed is all about women. About honoring and remembering the ancient matriarchal culture wisdoms. About honoring Mother Earth and her gifts. About honoring the sacred menstrual cycles. Moon cycles. She encourages women to stand naked and proud and let their moon-blood drip back into Mother Earth and nourish her soil. Wow! What the hell is that? I grimaced. Shocking! Shocking at first, but then somehow, I really like it. It reeks of "I am goddess, a giver of life." Girl power! It set my torch ablaze. Geez, I think I just singed my bangs!!

Susun is all about nourishment. Simple nourishment. She says scientific medicine is not about healthcare, but about disease-care. And the "heroic" tradition (aka, alternative medicine) focuses too much on cleansing and blame. I never liked blame; it always causes angst.

To illustrate these traditions, think of a tomato plant. Now, say its leaves are yellow and limp, and it has little or no fruit. Scientific farming would test the soil, add chemical fertilizer, and spray with pesticide. The heroic method would deem the plant weak, and replace the soil with raw-food vegan fertilizer. Then sprinkle some crushed vitamin supplements on the leaves, and also do a high-colonic inside the fruits.

A wise-woman would simply nourish that plant by adding some nice dark humus-filled natural soil and water. Then strong green leaves would begin to shoot out all over, and the fruit would become ripe and heavy. The winds may blow, but the strong stalks would be flexible in the gusts.

How is it that we, who are natural creatures of this planet (just as a tomato) do not understand what is good "soil" or nourishment for us? Why is it that we have lost touch with where our food comes from, what is good for nourishment, and what are empty calories with little or no nutritional value? Is it not the most important thing we can know?

Why is it that we do not know anymore that one only has to turn to the nearest white pine tree and pick one five-needle clump and eat it, to receive the daily recommended dose of vitamin C? Perhaps it is because free food does not make anyone rich. Hmm, let me think about that for a minute. What do *you* think? Choosing simple nourishing foods is one of the most important choices you and I can make for our health. Imagine if the vast majority of people were healthy. How would that change the world? The social, political, and emotional impacts are just too huge to grasp. But I can start with me, and you can start with you, and we can see how it goes.

Meeting Susun Weed has enamored me to change my soil back to the simple and authentic gifts from Mother Earth, and to honor my feminine energy more. I will study the Wise Woman way. Hey, don't knock it. If the economy completely collapses, I will be able to live off the land! I will brew the medicinal vinegars, steep my nettle infusion, and serve it all up with a dandelion salad topped with pretty red clover blossoms. As I take these gifts from Mother Earth, I will thank her and the plant spirits. And for dessert, if I want, I will also occasionally eat an entire box of Fiddle-Faddle. My strong and flexible system will be able to take the occasional Fiddle-Faddle storm.

Susun closed her talk with a song, and it went like this:

"It's time
To be the goddess now
It's time to be the goddess now.
It's time, it's time, it's time, it's time
It's time to be the goddess now."

I swear I am not making this up!

Fest by the Lake

Susun's talk was held outside at a state park during an early fall festival. I had really wanted to see her and decided that a festival setting of "Pagan Pride Day" would not deter me. Pagan is a scary word to me, and I am not sure why. The more I thought about that, the more curious I got, since it was billed as a family-friendly day. The Web site invited all Wiccans, Druids, Celtics, Fairies, Divas, and Vampires. Interesting. I can barely even define any of these traditions, but since I was a random goddess, I thought I would fit right in with these earth peoples. Plus it might make a good story. And it does, so read on, my voyeuristic friend.

True to the invite, all walks came. Mostly the people were nothing out of the ordinary. Singles, couples, families. About ten percent wore outfits that would fit right in at King Arthur's medieval faire: full length gypsy skirts with tight fitted bodices and plump, spilling bosoms, flower garland crowns, ribbons of every color, or shoulder capes made of fur. It was beautiful to see those enchanting folks moving through the forest as they went from workshop areas to stage areas to vendor areas. I felt as if I stood a good chance of spotting Robin Hood and Maid Marian on a sunny stroll.

Although not everyone was wearing it, black seemed to be the popular color of the day. Upon closer inspection, I noticed that the great majority of folks were wearing a silver necklace with a pagan star. Now, this festival was held less than an hour north of the infamous Salem, Massachusetts. So that means there was quite a bit of witch and warlock garb nearby to be easily had. Possibly fifteen percent of the attendees sported accoutrements such as full length capes, pointed black hats, black leather and buckles, and black fishnets. The Wiccans in black did not stir such romantic feelings as the Druids and Divas, but were fun to see. (I must admit that my favorite Halloween costume to wear is the witch outfit. I have donned that outfit many times on October 31st.) My favorite scary guy had written a book on vampires, and was strutting around in an outfit that would look great on the Harry Potter movie set. Actually, this guy did look very much like an older professor Snape: from his massive black leather and multi-buckled boots, past his silver ring encrusted fingers that were clenched on the metal topper of his shiny black walking stick, to his frilly white shirt and velvet vest. I almost wanted to strike up a conversation with him, but I didn't dare. He was so unusual that I wanted to get a feel for his vibe, to look in his eyes. But alas, it was not to be. He was very popular that day, and always surrounded by a crowd. (Plus, I was afraid that if I looked into his eyes he would get me in a Vulcan mind meld.)

After the weed walk, deciding not to wait in line at the food tents, I went shopping at the vendor tents instead. I toyed with possibly purchasing all the makings to dress as a medieval wench (probably would have had to make a trip to Frederick's of Hollywood to find some matching undergarments) and trying out my new look on Jake by candlelight over some venison and beer. But alas, that was not to be either. I wasn't there to buy clothes, I was there for the weed lesson.

But it never hurts to browse. The vendors were selling my old friends from the mineral kingdom, the crystals I spoke of before: my lucky charms. That was just the start of the interesting wares. There were books on all topics, from herbs to vampires. There were magic wands and brooms made of gnarled wood, all kinds of magical clothes, capes, and headdresses. The strangest headdress was made to look like

a giant black crow's head and beak, complete with feathers. It rides low and covers most of the face. Intimidating mask, it scared me a little.

There were also pendulums, incense, jewelry galore, books, figurines, creams, and loose herbs. I purchased a bag of chamomile for tea, and then also a bag of myrrh – because I had never seen it before and I know it was one of the Three Wise King's gifts to the baby in the manger. Gifting them to myself, I would add them to my collection of herbs that had finally arrived via UPS. What luck!

I purchased Susun Weed's book "Healing Wise", and she autographed it with a flourishing "Green Blessings" and her signature. I began my home study of herbs in earnest that very night. I was highly interested in cooking her dandelion autumn dish, for starters, or brewing some dandelion wine. Which I brewed up the following spring. It was delicious! It tastes like a white wine spritzer, and was fun to make.

RECIPE: Dandelion Wine

(From Susun Weed's "Healing Wise")

Dandelion Wine à la Laughing Rock
Our year's supply for rituals and medicine
2gal/8 liter crock
3-5 qts/3-5 liters blossoms
5 qts/5 liters water
3 pounds/1.5 kg sugar
1 organic orange
1 organic lemon
1 pkg/8 grams live yeast whole wheat bread toast

DIRECTIONS:

Find a field of dandelions in bloom on a glorious shining day. Follow the honeybees to the finest flowers. Pick them with a sweeping motion of your parted fingers, like a comb. I leave the green sepals on, but get rid of all stalks.

Back home, put blossoms immediately into a large ceramic, glass or plastic vessel. Boil water; pour over flowers. Cover your crock with cheesecloth. Stir daily for three days. On the fourth day strain blossoms from liquid.

Cook liquid with sugar and rind of citrus (omit rind if not organic) for 30-60 minutes. Return to crock. Add citrus juice. When liquid has cooled to blood temperature, soften yeast, spread on toast, and float toast in crock. Cover and let work two days. Strain.

Return liquid to crock for one more day to settle. Filter into very clean bottles and cork lightly. Don't drink until winter solstice.

Preparation time: A week's worth of effort yields a drink not only delightful but good for your liver, as well.

♀ Torch Time 6 ♀

Put a tiki-torch out in the herb garden at dusk and relax. Watch the moon rise while smelling the healing scents all around you. Take this time to slow way down, and focus on healing and pampering your body:

Meet the goddess: Kuan Yin is the Eastern goddess of compassion. She urges you to be kind and gentle to yourself and others. How would Kuan Yin mediate a debate between your floating angel and devil, so that everybody wins? Use her voice to guide you.

1. Breathe in and out, slowly, seven times right now. What do you experience? How do you feel?

_____

_____

_____

_____

2. How many cups of coffee or caffeinated tea/soda do you drink a day?

_____

_____

_____

_____

Decaffeinate yourself and slow down. Go on an herbal tea spree! Explore the effects of different teas.

3. Have you ever used natural hand-made soaps with herbs?

_____

_____

_____

_____

What a treat! You will never go back. Make some or buy some. Check the internet for how to do this.

4. Bath time! Fill up the tub, light a candle, and take a hot bath with your new herby friends Ms. Steaming Tea and Ms. Slippery Soap. Breathe slowly. Think back to the angel/devil exercise on page 27. Try to see the argument from various points of view. Feel exactly where this conflict manifests itself in your physical body. Focus on that location, and then visualize golden healing light immersing the muscles and tissue. Let the tension, from carrying that conflict around within you, dissipate into the warm water. Pull the plug and let it flow away down the drain with the bathwater. Be kind to yourself.

Autumn Comes and Leaves

My walks around the drumlin lake began to take on a different feel as summer turned to fall. Water drew back from the shore, exposing pipes and muck. The once submerged roots of the bushy trees were now exposed. The dragonflies did not linger in the glade anymore. Plants and weeds directed their energy away from the leaves and flowers, and into their roots and seeds. As the understory began to die down, in the grape scented air, the leaves in the canopy began their spectacular show. I remembered back to last autumn, when I first fell in love with the drumlin lake. In early October of the previous year, I had taken the plunge, moved from the village to the valley, and signed my very first solo mortgage. Happy and excited, scared and insecure, I sought refuge and peace in walks around the nearby lake. Perfect timing, as the forest was at its most beautiful exactly then.

One of my favorite trails of the autumn is up over a small hill, through a narrow trail lined with leafy trees that blot out the sky. Golden leaves are set on fire by the sun above, and appear in sacred glow when viewed from the path below. Daily they started to drop, one by one: happy yellow angels floating by. The next week they fell like raindrops, covering the path and giving the walker with that delightful "crunch-crunch." At the height of the leaves' pilgrimage to the forest floor, so many leaves were flowing by that it evokes the feeling in the walker of swimming through a school of millions of tiny bright yellow fish. Breathtaking.

At the peak of the small hill, and just on the downslope, are two very large trees that are starting to fall. They are right against each other, and are keeping each other up. I think of those two trees as an ancient married couple, who are living for each other right until the end. One cannot survive without the other. And indeed, if one of those old trees should fall all the way down some stormy night, the other will not be standing either. Til death do us part.

A strong and perfect "X" is formed by those two trees. Like the vaulted ceiling of a small cathedral, the X rises tens of feet above shoulder height. The soft and narrow path continues directly under this X of love. This X marks a spot. Pause under it and make your wish, express your gratitude, or perhaps just smile and expand your vibration. Breathe the holy golden air and wonder what it would feel like to be a tree. Wonder about destiny and free will. Wonder about loyalty and love. Wonder about the other half of your X.

Next year, on the second anniversary of my new home in the valley, I hope to see that old X still standing firm. This year, on my first anniversary, the X remains, offering me life-lessons as I happily pass under it. So many simple blessings. Orgasmagical, indeed.

The Labyrinth

That same fall, as the leaves floated and danced in the darkened October sky, our monthly Full Moon Meditation group took place outside on a newly constructed labyrinth in the yard at the farm. Ten silent men and women, each holding a small round votive, walked single file slowly around the edge of the pond and continuing on towards the far edge of the property. The crisp air echoed the song of the swaying trees, light with their bountiful bouquet of colored leaves. The pines whispered in harmony. The full moon illuminated all in an unearthly blue glow. It was a glorious evening. It was Van Morrison's " magical night for a moondance," with the stars up above in that October sky. Can't you just hear the cello? Fantabulous!

The walkers stopped at a large boulder, placed a few yards away from the entrance to the labyrinth. Under one corner of the craggy boulder, rested a metal bowl holding a white sage smudging torch. The torch was lit and its fragrance filled the air in curlicue wisps. In Native American tradition, each person was smudged, or encircled with white sage smoke, to bring forth blessings. I was smudged by the woman in front of me, then I turned to smudge Faith, who was behind me. I felt honored to smudge my sister goddess.

Thus blessed, we continued on our journey to the labyrinth entrance. A small CD player now drifted the magical, mystical sounds of Native American instruments through the chilly air. We circled around the outside of the labyrinth first, each one of us setting down our votive ten feet from the next to form a glowing ring. The center of the labyrinth held a large party torch. The inner and the outer flames worked in concert to dimly light the brick pathways.

Labyrinths are spiritual tools that calm and focus the mind. There are many ways and reasons to walk a labyrinth. As you walk, you can focus on a topic, a problem, or just one word. You can walk in silence. You can chant. There are multitudes of ways to use this tool. Tonight's walk was to inaugurate and dedicate the newly constructed labyrinth. Natalie and Bill, the owners of the farm, began to speak of their new labyrinth. They told of how the dimensions were planned, of obtaining the bricks from Freecycle, and of the helpers that pieced it all together. They told of their joy at the reality of it, and of the immense happiness in sharing it with us, their friends. Natalie then said a prayer of thanksgiving, instructed us to each focus on our own inner question or topic, and then she stepped onto the first bricks. We each followed, ten feet after the person in front of us.

When it was my turn, I stepped in silently. Rounding the first outer ring, I was surprised by a large toad that jumped away from in front of me and off to hide in the deep shadows under the balsam pines. Ah, yes, an animal totem. What luck! The message of the toad is good luck and prosperity. How auspicious to be sent a message from the toad.

As I slowly made my way into the center of the labyrinth, I thought with gratitude about the past year and how blessed I had been. The needles of a white pine kissed my forehead as I drifted by. I felt intense gratitude for the past year and my spiritual growth. Walking slowly helps the mind to focus on the essence of the topic. Shadows of other walkers passed by me in random fashion but they did not distract, I kept my eyes down, intent and focused on the shadowy bricks and the shadowy past. The others were very focused also. It was intense.

Finally, all ten of us stood silently in the center, faces shining in the flame of the torch, while behind us clouds shone majestically by the light of the full harvest moon. Joining hands for a prayer, I focused on Natalie. She spoke with emotion, her breath caught in the chilly air and formed shapes as she spoke. She asked that we keep this place, this moment, within our hearts. "When you begin to feel alone in the world, remember that you are not. Remember this moment, inside this circle. Remember being safe and loved and blessed."

After a moment of silence, the first walkers began to wind their way out. It takes just as long to get out of a labyrinth as it does to get in. One premise of the ancient labyrinth is that you find your answer in the center or just leave your problem/obstacle there. On the way out you strategize future plans. The center of a labyrinth can function like a giant trash can. Symbolically leave your problem there, and boom, you are free to move on!

Tonight's walk was not about problems for me, though. My topic was gratitude. Have you ever focused on feeling all aspects of gratitude? Try it! When I got to the center I was so happy. Before I left the center, I turned and gave Faith a giant hug of appreciation and love. I was so happy to stand in the center with my sister goddess. The walk out of the labyrinth was done without my feet touching the ground, or at least it felt that way!

Orbs

Winter came again, my least favorite time of year. Ugh. However, in the spirit of the goddess Aphrodite, I tried to find and celebrate the joy in winter. For the past four decades I had complained myself through it to anyone in earshot. This year would be different, Mother Earth and the Winds of the North were now my kin.

Celeste had an extra pair of snowshoes and invited me out for an early winter walk along the valley riverbank. Stepping from my car, I pulled my hat down over my ears, and strapped on the snowshoes. They felt very odd at first, but then my gait adjusted and soon we were trucking right along through the woods. We passed through a field littered with rabbit tracks. They criss-crossed each other in a mad swirl, whirling all about the field.

Here and there was a very odd sight that I had trouble figuring out at first. Turned out to be wing prints of a bird that had a wingspan of about three or four feet. The tips of the wings were outlined feather by feather. It was quite striking. I wondered why a bird would leave its wing prints on the ground again and again. I soon enough figured it out. Can you guess? Nature in action. A hawk swoops down and gets a rabbit. Its powerful wings bash against the ground as it lifts from the ground, heavy with its dinner! Poor little bunny foo-foo.

Down by the riverbank all was frozen. The mighty Merrimack River, born hundreds of miles away in the White Mountains, is only ten miles from the sea when it races through my valley. It was so cold that the river was frozen over solid. Regardless, I enjoyed that walk tremendously, my first outside walk in months. (The treadmill at the gym is nowhere near as scenic). When it started to get dusky, we headed back to the cars.

We passed across the rabbit field again, and I wanted to stop and hide behind a bush to see if a rabbit would pass by. We squished up under a bush, like a couple of lunatics. The snowshoes made it difficult to sit comfortably, and we were splayed out all a-kimbo in the manner of tossed mannequins. Trying to be totally silent we watched for the approach of any rabbits. We watched for a while, but the wabbits were too wiley. They were probably laughing at our splayed spectacle from the safety of their little burrows. But, although the rabbit peeping was unsuccessful, the time spent in silence served to calm us down into a peaceful state of mind. We finally unscrunched out from under the bush and shook our legs out.

Celeste wanted to stop and take some digital pictures. She said she had taken some pictures there before, near dusk, and they had shown up with orbs in them.

"What is an orb?" I asked.

"A little globe of light. You can't see it when you look at the field now, but after I take the picture we may see it in the camera screen. Let's take some and see what we get."

Pulling off her gloves, she reached into her parka pocket, and started fiddling with a camera. I turned in a full circle (hard to do with snowshoes on) and looked all around the field I had just been staring at for the last twenty minutes in my rabbit quest. I saw no lights. Celeste had gotten the camera working, and was snapping away in all directions.

"Come, look into the camera and see if we got anything."

I snowshoed over, and tried to get close to her without having my snowshoes land on top of hers. After I somewhat successfully negotiated this, I leaned in and peered into the screen of the digital camera she held up. She was moving through the shots one by one. And there they were, I recognized them immediately. The same little light blobs that I had caught dancing around Jewell's head at her birthday party. Angels! Spirits! Light Beings! Whatever you want to call them, they were clearly in the shots. I squinted and looked slowly around again at the field. There were no street lamps or headlights or any unnatural light for a mile. Very interesting.

Could there be scientific reason for this illusion? Dew in the air? Microscopic fleas? Cosmic dust? I don't know, but it is much more fun to think of them as light-beings or fairies of some sort. I have a print of an old classic painting hanging in my bedroom. In sepia-like tones, it depicts a young girl in a moonlit forest, bending over to talk to the tiny wood sprites and fairies. The tiny contingent glows in a festive circle, in the grass beneath her gathered skirts. In the background, there are orbs.

"This area on the riverbank is supposed to be an old Native American site, now it is conservation land. Let's call for the orbs, invite them to come, and then take more pictures," Celeste said.

We both were silent; the goddess Ixchel, and the goddess Aphrodite, standing together in a frozen field at dusk, asking politely to see the lights once again. With my eyes closed, I breathed my wish and then I smiled "as if." She took another picture. It was filled with many, many little orbs. A sparkly soiree of specters? Boomshaka-lucka! I couldn't believe it. It was truly fantastic. I asked if I could take a picture of her in the field. She passed me the camera, and I stepped back a bit and took her picture. It shows Celeste in the field, small orbs around her, and one really big one with a kind of streak coming down out of it, right up in the front of the screen. It's a keeper. (If you want to see orbs for yourself, search the word "orb" online.)

These Woods are Snowy, Dark, and Deep

Winter continued, interspersed this year with many moments of chilly joy. One February day, the weathermen had issued a winter storm advisory. The storm was to begin after lunch and be a classic New England blizzard. Here in New England there are different names for different kinds of storms. This was no small squall, no moderate snowfall, no whizzing Alberta Clipper. This was the full out biggun' they were predicting: a Nor'Easter. Batten down the hatches, fill up the water jugs, rush the supermarkets for storm food and batteries, get your flashlight and candles at the ready; here it comes.

I left work early, and got home just before the heaviest part of the storm was predicted to begin. Tucking my car safely in the garage, I ran upstairs and quickly popped a roast in the oven, and went right back down cellar to suit up. Then, I doused my goddess torch with a double shot of gasoline, and I went out to play!

Looking like an Arctic adventurer, I stepped out the cellar door, and into the wonderland of silent tiny flakes. Tiny and perfect, and oh so many of them! They were coming down straight, no wind to blow them into my face, and there were so many that the visibility was very gray. Actually when there is that much snow in the afternoon, I find the world appears to have almost a light blue tint. Blue, gray, call it what you want, it was marvelous, and it enveloped me in snowy, muffled, quietness. *It's time. . . to be the goddess now, it's time to be the goddess now . . .*

There was already three inches on the ground when I stepped outside, and when I got back to my door, an hour and a half later, there was eight inches. It was snowing straight down like crazy! It was snowing a great kind of snow, too: tiny squeaky flakes that are good for snowballs, snowmen, and sliding. As I walked I kicked my steps out in front of me just for the fun of seeing it explode off my boot tip into giant pom-poms of white. The unplowed streets were silent, in fact the streets had disappeared into the lawns, which had disappeared into the surrounding pine forest. All was one expanse as far as the eye could see. The snowy blanket had turned the clock back two hundred years.

My plan was to make a complete circle just inside the edge of the forest around the entire complex, see what there was to experience, and then exit where I came in. It seemed like a safe plan, and that I would be back home in a half hour or less. I was wrapped up in gore-tex from head to foot, but had left a two-inch opening for my eyes. Through this slit I spied a small opening at the edge of the lawn that led into the forest.

Pine boughs laden with snow formed a perimeter wall, but for that small opening. Pushing myself through, the boughs joyously unloaded their fluffy burden on me. I loved it! Inside the forest all was very calm, so calm I could hear the bristly noises the snow made as each flake bumped against each other in their haste to their chosen resting spot. The pine smelled wonderful. I decided to eat some white pine needles. They tasted like the best Christmas ever. I set off on my clockwise journey past the pines and birches. Looking back to the condos from a small ridge behind the screen of the trees was quite pleasant. It was as if I were inside a giant snow globe of a tiny village. Just snow and trees and house, but no people—maybe the soft glow of a light on a distant window to suggest people, but no actual people or cars to be seen. An interesting illusion from my hidden trail on the ridge, peeking out occasionally from behind the great sheltering pines.

About halfway around, the pines gave way to a small stretch to a scrubby field on the edge of the wood. Passing through there I saw my old friends, the weeds, their carcasses dried and bent. The milkweeds bowed to the snow, and danced with it. The intertwined grasses puckered together in heavy tufted bunches and their rounded heads were topped with fluffy white caps. I knew their roots were safely underground, gossiping with each other, gathering energy for their big springtime comeback. I know the plant spirits speak to those who can hear. But for now, although I want to be able to, I still cannot hear their whispers. Dang! I tromped on and re-entered the forest through another break in the pines, a much larger path. I followed it for a while, then decided I was getting too far away, and turned back.

On the way back I decided that instead of ducking under the snowy boughs and not disturbing them, that I would run and leap and let them dump all over me just for fun. I skipped, I jumped, I stood directly under the biggest branches I could find and gave a big yank. Avalanche on my head. An avalanche of blessings. Giggling, I did it again and again, uninhibited like a child. I skipped around some more, and sang some little songs. I made up songs to Frost's "These woods are snowy, dark, and deep . . ." My inner child was in full bloom. Playing is very therapeutic! I think I shall play like a child more often, and suggest you try it, too.

Leaving the snowy path, I crossed the lawn and entered the woods again behind the well pump-house. I had been there in the fall. There is a clearing about a hundred yards in that is surrounded by a ring of big pines. In the center are thick, but neat brambles and bushes, with small winding paths through them, mostly dead ends. I know deer and rabbits must sleep under the brambles. There is a small pond quite near, just outside the ring of pines. On an earlier visit in the fall, I was astounded at the number of birds who played in the clearing. They barely even noticed me, as they went about their chasing games. They were so vocal. I don't think I had ever heard so much bird chatter. It was loud. It was delightful. But those birds had either flown south now, or were hiding away from this storm. The quietness was loud today.

By now, an hour had passed since I started out, and the snow was still falling rapidly and oppressively. It was just starting to become a shade dusky. I punched my way into the clearing, and sat down on a small path beside a bramble patch. Slowly I began to breathe in and out. I meditated for a while, and tried my best to commune with this wondrous snowfall, that poured down over every inch of me. I tried to be the snowfall, the atmosphere. Time stood still. Smiling and laying back flat, I made a snow angel (oops! I mean a snow-goddess), then lay still, just under the lacy brambles above. The snow fell right onto my face, and melted into rivulets that dripped away like tears of joy. I had made friends with Mother Nature's snowy side, at long last.

It was time to head back. All the way back out of the woods I pulled on every branch and got many avalanches of snow blessings dropped on my head. The snow was so deep now. Running sluggishly across the lawn in the deep snow, I dropped just before my front steps and made one last snow-goddess for all to see. The light was really fading now, and the street lamps were casting a pinkish glow on the still unplowed street. It is a sight rarely seen, sunset through the snow storm, and I happened to be in the right place at the right time. What luck!

Stopping in front of the cellar door, I tried to stamp all the caked snow off me that I could. I was really mounded up like the Abominable Snowman. Oh well, the stiff clothing would melt once inside the cellar, no harm. I was tired from all the playing, so still mounded up with snow, inside I went to throw my snowman suit on the floor. The wafting aroma of roasting pork greeted me as I opened the door. Now that is what I call a happy winter ending! It was to be the last big storm of that winter, and I was looking forward to spring equinox and Beltane.

Take Back Beltane

The more in synch I get with my simple spirituality, and my goddessness, the more I feel tied to the rhythms of Mother Earth and the orbiting cycles of the planets, as detailed in the *Farmer's Almanac*. I love both the full moon and the new moons. Very powerful times. Times you want to drink dandelion wine and howl at the moon by the light of your torch, just for fun!

If you remember back, dear reader, you will note that the "first crack in my cosmic egg" took place on a spring equinox. There are two equinoxes each year, one in the spring and one in the fall. At these times of the year there are exactly as many hours in the day as there are in the night. Another cosmic event is the solstice. There are two solstices: the longest day of the year (summer solstice), and the shortest day of the year (winter solstice). Very meaningful to me is that my youngest daughter was born on the winter solstice, the day also celebrated as the "return of the light."

Are you a visual person? I am, so let me paint a picture to explain this. Imagine a round clock. Noon is the longest day of the year (summer solstice) and six o'clock is the shortest day of the year (winter solstice). Three o'clock is when daylight hours again are equal in length to nighttime hours (the fall equinox). And nine o'clock is when daylight hours equal nighttime hours (the spring equinox). Isn't that handy? But wait, there is a little bit more!

Now, continuing with the clock metaphor, there are four more points on this circle, points that you may or may not have heard of. Halfway between summer solstice and autumn equinox, in September (on the clock it would be 1:30) is Lammas, the harvest feast. Exactly halfway between the fall equinox and the winter solstice (at 4:30) is a special point we call All Hallow's Eve, or Halloween. It is derived from the ancient Celtic holiday of Samhain, and I am sure it has it's roots in ritual even more ancient than that. It is the time that the last of the crops go to bed for the season, the time to rest through the wintry winds, the time of the dead. After the winter solstice, in February (at 7:30) is Imbolic, the feast of the flames, when spring just begins to draw near. Directly opposite All Hallow's, (at 10:30) is life and being born from out of the ground. This is May 1, May Day, the day known to the ancient Celts as Beltane.

Both Lammas and Imbolic have been all but erased from mainstream celebration, as Christianity does not like these earth-based holidays, but Samhain and Beltane (renamed) continue on as curious oddities in our culture. But what could be more natural as a being of this planet, than to celebrate the rhythms of the earth and its fruits? Be green. Be a green goddess! Let the *Old Farmer's Almanac* be your bible!

At Halloween,you know you are getting outside at night for one of the last times before the cold really settles in and the ground freezes. I like Halloween because it is fun to take on a completely different persona for the night, and make other people laugh. Like that time at the ballroom Halloween party when I dressed as a medieval princess, complete with a pointy princess hat, and was waltzing with a man in a full gorilla suit. What a visual! I think I am a little biased towards Halloween, because I was born inside the Halloween week.

But my true favorite is May Day, or Beltane. What a joyous day! I think we should bring it back in full force. It is truly an earth-based holiday for goddesses. It is the day ruled over by the Celtic goddesses Cordelia and Aine. Aine is the "Queen of the Fairies," She oversees spring fertility and flowers. Every little sleeping sprite wakes up from its wintry nook on May Day. Look in an asparagus bed if you don't believe me! You will see all kinds of little green heads poking up from thawing wintery gardens. Showy daffodils, stately irises, spunky chives, and even granny rhubarb in her big green housecoat uncovers her head and turns her wrinkly face to the Beltane sunlight.

Next May Day make a plan to dance a jig around a Maypole with your goddess friends. Make a plan to frolic in a field of fresh dandelions surrounded by lilac bushes. Oh, what a heavenly scent! Can't you smell it now? Weave a Maycrown of field flowers and hold court over the butterflies and bees, with the crickets as jesters. Put a basket of fresh picked flowers on your neighbor's doorstep, ring the bell, and run away. Let's give May Day back its true name, Beltane, and put it back on the calendars. Make a plan to celebrate May Day like the true goddess you are.

As it just so happens, my older daughter was born on May Day. She was two weeks overdue, but apparently she was just waiting for her true date of arrival. And you know what card was drawn for her "persona" card from the magical goddess deck on her nineteenth birthday? Take a leap of faith. You guessed it! Aine, Queen of the Fairies: What luck!

⚝ Torch Time 7 ⚝

Twirl your torch like a flaming baton, keep your flame burning bright through play. Find wonder and joy every day. Run and jump and spin until you are out of breath. Smile and giggle and shout!

Meet the goddess: Cordelia is the Celtic Queen of the May Day flowers. She encourages you to recognize the need for more play in your life and invites you to go outside and play. A daily venture outside will revive your soul and spirit. And you just may get Boom shaka-lucky while you are out there frolicking!

1. Write about the last time you went outside and played

_____

_____

_____

_____

Arrange to do it again very soon. If you have forgotten how to play, visit a local park and watch the four-year-olds in action.

2. Have you ever celebrated Beltane?

_____

_____

_____

_____

Research it or not, but do throw a raucous party on May 1 for you and your goddess friends. Play with abandon in the flowers. Dance around a Maypole. If Beltane is too far away, plan a party for the next full moon. Check the _Old Farmer's Almanac_ for a moon schedule.

3. Go to a bookstore or online and buy your own deck of goddess cards. Play with them over and over until they are truly yours and they begin to "speak" to you.

The Sacred Art of Inspiration

One morning I woke up to a voice that sounded like a woman standing directly beside my bed. The ethereal woman, whom I never did see, spoke only one sentence. She spoke so clearly that I looked to see who was in my empty room. Nobody. Gently and firmly, she said as plain as day this phrase: "The sacred art of inspiration." So, my friends, that is how this book was born— through a dream.

This peaceful, loving goddess-simpler would practice the sacred art of inspiration by holding herself up as a mirror. Look into me and my life, warts and all, and see if you can find a reflection of yourself. Learn from my adventures and mis-adventures. Look into the goddess cards and see if you can grow your intuition. Look into yourself, your simple self, breathe, and then follow your bliss.

I am hoping that through the adventurous, humorous, and bittersweet tales in this book, you will be inspired to awaken, to enlighten your torch and yourself, and to see your own way to awareness, peace, and bliss. Myself, I am looking to stay calm, sure, and orgasmagical . . . and Boom shaka-lucky. Spirit is flashin' in me! Take me higher. Boom, boom!

In conclusion, my dear sister goddesses and friends, I hope you have enjoyed the frolics held within these pages. The journey continues in earnest now. Spring has once again sprung! Walt Whitman's long brown path stretches before us, leading wherever we choose. The journey could be smooth. The journey could be rough. But either way it offers us new prizes. These are the days that must happen to us.

All goddesses, now raise your lucky torches high. *Allons!* Where shall we go next?

The end.

. . . or the beginning . . .

Your choice!

About the Author

R. M. Allen is a green goddess who lives simply in Southern New Hampshire, and works in a very traditional church office in a quintessential New England village. She holds a masters degree in business communications, and is on orgasmagical spiritual safari. The combination of all of the above contributes to her fun and unique writing style, which is inspiring to her sister goddesses. Find out more at www.NHgoddess.com